A Story about Mr. Silberstein

A Story about Mr. Silberstein

Erland Josephson

Translated from the Swedish
by Roger Greenwald

Northwestern University Press
Evanston, Illinois

Hydra Books
Northwestern University Press
Evanston, Illinois 60208-4210

Published 2001 by Northwestern
University Press. First published in
Swedish by Albert Bonniers förlag
as *En berättelse om herr Silberstein.*
Copyright © 1957 by Erland
Josephson. English translation
copyright © 1995 by Roger
Greenwald. First published 1995
by Northwestern University Press.
All rights reserved.

Printed in the United States
of America

10 9 8 7 6 5 4 3 2 1

ISBN 0-8101-1910-2

Library of Congress
Cataloging-in-Publication Data

Josephson, Erland, 1923–
  [Berättelse om herr Silberstein.
English]
  A story about Mr. Silberstein /
Erland Josephson ; translated from
the Swedish by Roger Greenwald.—
[2nd ed.]
    p. cm.
  "Hydra books."
  ISBN 0-8101-1910-2 (pbk. : alk.
paper)
    I. Title: Story about Mister Sil-
berstein. II. Greenwald, Roger, 1945–
III. Title.
PT9875.J66 B4713 2001
839.73'74—dc21

                        2001026606

CONTENTS

TRANSLATOR'S NOTE

I would like to thank Erland Josephson for his invaluable help with this translation, and Sylvia Söderlind for advice about the Swedish.

My thanks go as well to those who read drafts and offered criticism and suggestions. Of the many people who have offered encouragement and practical aid, I would like to mention Dorotea Bromberg and Jenny Pedersen of Brombergs Bokförlag, Leif Sjöberg, Lars Malmström, Elisabeth Hall, Gunilla Forsén, Helen Sigeland, Joan Tate, Rika Lesser, and Marna Feldt.

I am grateful to the National Endowment for the Arts and to the Swedish Institute for grants that assisted me in my work.

This translation is dedicated to Daryl Fridenberg.

. . . and stopped in front of the only building on the block that hadn't been torn down; it was the corner building, and the street sign on it showed what the block had been called when it was a whole block: The Mirage (Schoolmaster Olausson liked to say: Symbolic name – the housing shortage!). And it was in front of this building that the vehicle stopped and it was quite plainly a truck and there was quite plainly a load of belongings on the flatbed.

A miserable truckload. The load that had pulled away – the old accountant's things (dead, dead and almost no one had ever seen him) – had been unremarkable but at least worth looking over. This stuff: worn but not broken, not new but not old, not exactly dirty but. . . . Bought at the auctioneer's, somebody said. Seen at the auctioneer's the other day, the whole lot, on inspection, someone else added. That's right (a third).

And the tenant? that lucky stiff who'd succeeded in getting hold of the two-room apartment. Presumably the man who was sitting next to the driver – a slouch hat hid his face – and who stayed there when the entrance door was propped open, when the apartment door was unlocked, when the movers began to unload, even when the flatbed was empty and the echoing had stopped in the stairwell.

Then you could see: the hand being put into the dark and not very new ulster, the wallet, the bills being handed over, the door handle being pressed down. Further: that he was awkward climbing down, rather short and very odd-looking, of indeterminable age and in a hurry getting to the entranceway, and in a greater hurry on the stairs than he could really manage – you could hear huffing and puffing and an unsteady pace and the door slamming shut. Afterwards: silence, and nothing else, silence until you couldn't listen anymore, it's ill-mannered to press your ear against the silence; you could guess: had probably flung himself on the bed in the midst of all the junk, was surely lying there huddled up and staring at the ceiling. Or sleeping maybe.

Four storeys high on an otherwise empty lot, what was left of the block called The Mirage (symbolic name, according to the schoolmaster, think of the housing shortage – smiling). Would surely be torn down too, eventually, but the people? Housing shortage, of course. And until it was torn down nothing could be built anywhere on the block, but sooner or later: everybody out! Yet still a new tenant. Short reprieve. A lit-tle while we tar-ry here.*

There still wasn't a new nameplate, only the outline of the old one and the holes left by the screws, like the shadow of a man. And behind the door the quiet continued, no one had heard the sound of a suitcase being set on the floor or the scrape of a chair being moved. So you could just imagine the indescribable mess: everything where the moving men had put or thrown it, and in the middle of the floor perhaps the new arrival on his shabby mattress, maybe still in his overcoat, with his hands thrust deep into the pockets, and maybe with the slouch hat over his face so he breathed in the odors of sweaty forehead and unwashed hair.

Very tired, very weary, you might think and long to feel compassion, but instead maybe *oh shit* and *pigsty* or maybe *a hell of a lot of bottles.* But neither a sigh through the double floor in favor of one guess nor a clinking in favor of the other. Quiet.

No mail either. The mailman never asked Doesn't a certain So-and-So live in the building. Even though you asked the mailman if he didn't have someone to ask about? You'd swing past the door without a name, always very quick and indifferent, never hesitant.

---

*In a well-known Christmas song, this line is among those sung by the Christmas elves. – R. G.

In this way several days of our lives passed (and never came again)* but still nothing, nothing to grasp and keep hold of. But just you wait! Animals have to have food. You could just imagine him nibbling on a few moldy breadcrusts, or were the suitcases full of canned goods? A wholesaler of canned goods perhaps. But then surely you ought to have heard him swearing over the can-opener, or the swish when the bloody fingertips were rinsed clean in the washbasin.

Or maybe at night? Vanished from the house at night when other people were sleeping. In any case went to the privy then, because no one had heard that either.

No one heard him, no one saw him.

As Brundin said: He's a clever devil when it comes to making you curious.

So – three days of quiet, then suddenly the sounds you'd been waiting for, furious and as if all at once. Footsteps across the floor, packing cases being broken open, banging on the walls, nails, furniture sliding around, dishes clattering, pots clanging, water rushing in the pipes, the toilet flushing, even deep and heavy sighs were reported, coughing, hawking, mumbling, got up, sat down, something was dragged across the floor, maybe the bed, now something heavy, very heavy, must be that ugly bureau you'd seen, and finally, without anyone seeing when it was put up, the nameplate on the door, an exceptionally handsome nameplate of polished brass with wonderfully curlicued letters, the most beautiful letters in the whole stairwell:

SILBERSTEIN

Foreign. German. Or Austrian. Or Polish. German from Poland. Or Russian. German from Russia. Or Czech. Czech-German. Or

---

*The opening of this sentence is based on two lines from Psalm 434 in the Swedish Psalm Book. – R. G.

Austroczechotyrolean. Then again perhaps northern Italian. Swiss. Not French. Dutch. For that matter Olausson had met a Dane called Goldstein. So there we are. Out and out Swedish, then, perhaps.

Swedish name wearing a slouch hat.

It was best to wait for the face under the slouch hat. Then it would be a question of combining the face, the name and that strange hat.

Children's fingers on the elegant, shiny nameplate. The bolder ones rattled the top on the mailbox. But no footsteps approached. It had grown silent again.

People went around getting the feel of the name: Silberstine.

Not stine but shtine, said Olausson.

Damned snob!

The one who had the name, or the one who pronounced it that way? You didn't really know which one you'd meant.

Was seen at last, began at last to show himself. Raised that ugly hat politely to whomever he met on the stairs, even for the children he bared his bald crown and his lank black hair. His brow sloped back – as in animals, you might say – but under the strong eyebrows large dark-brown eyes with a gentle gaze – somewhat like a dog, you might think if you were sticking with the animals; the nose descended heavy and hooked, with fleshy nostrils extending down almost past the thick, moist lips that always seemed to tremble above the chin that curved in sharply toward the throat so the whole profile became an almost comical arc. The body thick-set and maybe a bit fat under the overcoat, hard to tell really, the legs short and the gait very careful and sort of flat, as if balancing were a risky venture. He smiled to almost everyone, it showed mostly in his eyes because he put his hand over his mouth then, no doubt to hide broken teeth whenever his lips parted.

Still not a single word, not even good-day or good-morning or good-afternoon, though you were waiting for the intonation and the accent, not even to the children though he often patted them on the head or the cheek; not after-you or excuse-me if you ran into him in the entranceway and nodded before and after, just the hat off and the left corner of his mouth shooting up behind his hand in that crooked smile that was perhaps frightened, perhaps kindly, perhaps nothing at all.

And no one got a glimpse into the apartment, the door never really opened wide, just enough for the thick body to squeeze through, turn around immediately and shut it again, and of course you couldn't go really close at those moments anyway.

He shook his head and smiled when the children rang and asked for old newspapers, he smiled and shook his head at peddlers and salesmen.

Perhaps understood nothing, perhaps understood everything. Perhaps understood too much, said one person.

A bitter one.

There were those who focused on his loneliness, longed for a feeling of it, a deep understanding. Such people longed to hear his voice more than others, wanted it to have a slight, soft accent that would represent isolation; to listen to it, to catch the impure sounds and then smiling gently: You don't have an accent at all, Mr. Silberstein, no one could believe anything but that you've lived in Sweden all your life. So fantasized Miss Svensson, for example.

Oh she could imagine: back from the library, come in for a cup of tea, Mr. Silberstein, no doubt you'd like to have someone to talk to (I have to find someone to talk to), you've surely gone through a great deal. How she would smile at him over the teacup (why couldn't she ever smile openly, like Louisa to name just one of the many who knew how to smile); how gently her hand would lift the cover off the candy jar from which she had, in advance, removed all the toffees – which she herself doted on – so as not to remind the lonely man of his poor teeth, only small round hard candies in cheerful colors to suck on gracefully in the dusk. And later all the intimate conversations, everything that she – no, that *he* – would tell of, he must certainly have many dead relatives, all his dear ones were dead, perhaps, or very far away, across the seas. So all about this and all about that, and afterwards much more, about life, about people, the wicked and the good, in the evenings that were so heavy otherwise, when your gaze began to wander across the page and the pressure in your breast tormented you.

Oh she could see it all and hear it all in such beautiful daydreams in the evening, so lovely that she disconcertedly passed her rough hand across her forehead, smoothing away the strands of prematurely gray hair that were tickling her eye. Poor man, she whispered, but didn't achieve the compassion she yearned for, there was a cold draft from the window. For his sake, she strained, for his sake, but couldn't keep hold of it, and later, in her sleep, she wreaked a terrible vengeance on herself: his loathsome face came close to hers, his sour breath blew into her nostrils, she looked into the gaping red mouth with the thick tongue and the rotten stumps of teeth, and in this dream he hissed at her in a horrible patois:

I vant to be poysecuted!

Others derived great pleasure from the hard fate he had suffered or avoided. Their pleasure too was propelled by compassion, but also by horror and disgust. The poor man, they said, you know of course what it was like in those camps he may have been in, no doubt you saw the films, you read the reports, you heard the witnesses. Imagine – soap made from the fat, lampshades from the skin, if you go to the theater you see their hair in the actors' wigs. Didn't you ever read about the packed freight-cars, they shit and screamed and died, stood squeezed together and shit and screamed and died. And the corpse-factories, naked and thin and no idea what was coming, the hunger and the lice and the ugly bodies, and all the blows and all the shots and all the kicks, haven't you read about it, haven't you seen the films – right, you've read about it, you've seen the films, so you know what I'm talking about and you too have heard about the soap and the lampshades and the actors' wigs and that they shit and screamed and died and were naked and thought they were going for showers, yes exactly! you see, the kicks and the shots and the blows and the hunger and the lice and do you remember anything else from all that horror? That's right! you're right about that, it was like that too and like that and like that. How humans can behave like that toward other humans – bastard Krauts, I've always called them, and I'll call them that as long as I live. You saw in the films how they carried on, didn't you, I'll never forget it, it's etched into my memory, poor bastards, like animals, feeling only hunger and cold and other such things that have nothing to do with thought and spiritual life.

But maybe this one got out earlier. Or maybe isn't from there at all. Hasn't spoken to a single person yet, after all. Maybe he's never seen a bastard Kraut.

In that case he has no reason to put on airs.

Has he put on airs, then?

No, but then he certainly has no reason to, does he.

Others loved each other under his auspices. They huddled together to protect themselves from the reality they thought he was, they lay in bed and whispered about him in the dark and got all heated up by what they supposed he'd been deprived of, everything cozy and secure, no one could take them away from each other.

Maybe he had a wife and children. Imagine. And now.

Maybe he saw them taken away.

Maybe saw them killed before his very eyes. My kitten.

Yes.

Maybe he had a fine home, owned fine things. You're sweet.

You too.

You're so soft. Perhaps they beat him terribly. Doesn't it seem to you that he has trouble walking?

Yes, he does. Your shoulder is so beautiful. I'm so comfortable like this. And his teeth. He must not have any teeth. You can just imagine.

To think that it happens. They're still people, after all. Hey, you're tickling me.

You've always been ticklish. Remember the beginning. I could hardly touch you.

Maybe I was a little afraid too. Do you think he's lying there now thinking about all that?

He probably can't sleep. Lies there staring at the ceiling.

Why can't they fix the place up? Even if it *is* gonna be torn down someday.

We've got to try and move.

He's been lucky, at any rate. If you think about all the others.

We've been lucky too.

Yes, if you think about him.

No, don't think about him. It's awful. I tell you it's awful.

Yes, but us. Dear.

Yes.

Where did he go when he went out? Quite regular these days, in fact: in the morning, disappeared down the street, at a pace that always seemed faster than he could really manage. Returned in the afternoon, slower, more sluggish, his chin hanging down, his mouth tired and slack, his shoulders seeming to slope even more, his coat seeming very heavy, his shoelaces trailing. He didn't have the strength to smile at the children who were playing Fugitive near the entranceway, he brought the game to a standstill and made the voices fall silent, one hand moved up out of his coat pocket in a slack gesture that might have been a wave, then dangled by his side, at a loss until it found something to do with the entrance door, a heavy sigh, the heavy door, a start when it slammed shut and the bang echoed emptily in the stairwell, then the big soft hand on the banister, a few seconds' hesitation before he started to climb up, step by step, tired, the keys that seemed to lie very deep in his pocket, the door with the incredibly beautiful nameplate, shut, and again this silence.

Where did he go when he went out? Perhaps he's getting ground up in that huge paper mill called the Bureaucracy, someone would say. No doubt collects money, they all stick together, he doesn't need to do a blessed thing (someone else). Not necessarily – it's quite possible that he works (a third). Takes a job from someone else in that case, is that fair? Never mind, there are enough for everyone, after all – at least so far. Or almost everyone. So? Maybe a little lending action on the side, certainly isn't unusual, with interest on the interest you don't do too badly. Well, he doesn't seem to be doing so great.

Where did he go when he went out? Follow him, kids! For no particular reason, but it'd be fun to know, after all. But for Chrissake be careful in the traffic! Well?

A little basement on the way downtown, a little basement shop but not a shop, a window but painted over in white so it wasn't a window, stairs from the street, just a few steps down to the door, that one also shut so quick you couldn't see anything.

All there was to know for the present, then.

Behavior pattern, said Schoolmaster Olausson, the man's behavior pattern. And smiled like one who knows for a certainty. Typical, he also said. The man's behavior pattern is typical. His silence is a symptom of an activated escape mechanism. For him, to speak would be to subject himself forcibly to the pressure of reality, since speaking is a means of contact and the man has had bad experiences from contact. Typical contact-inhibition.

He's probably just shy, someone said.

One can also express it that way if one wishes to simplify the picture in a case which at bottom is rather complicated, smiled the schoolmaster. Then seriously: Presumably a significant series of traumas he can't be blamed for is also a part of the essentials of the psychological picture. The man is sick, in any case, and the sick of course have a right to our forbearance.

Someone: Why forbearance? Has he done anything?

The schoolmaster smiled. Could it not be said that it is anti-social behavior to shut oneself off from all human contacts? What if everyone kept quiet, what if . . .

Someone: Might be nice.

Olausson was not the kind of person who couldn't appreciate a good joke, no indeed. And many were the times when he himself had felt that way. So nice to keep quiet. But in that case who would give the children an education? To take one example. What if everyone shut himself off from natural and necessary contacts. The grocery stores would close, the buses would stop running and so on and so on, in short the complex machinery of society, so hard for any one person to see in its entirety, would cease to function.

But maybe he just doesn't have a job where you need to talk.

By all means, by all means, but let us not be superficial now: even one's attitude toward those around one and toward society must be untainted by sabotage. A great French thinker spoke of the social contract.

But something criminal . . .

No, no, let's not get bogged down in trifles. It's important to think in terms of broad concepts.

But Silberstein . . .

That's just what I was saying: the man's behavior pattern suggests morbid disturbances caused by psychological injuries. We must show forbearance. Think of what he may have had to go through!

How ridiculous! Right on the top step, just when he was about to dig into his pocket for the doorkey, just when the late afternoon surge of people filled the stairs, the large bag he was carrying in his left hand burst. The red apples bounced and took off, and there he stood with a piece of crumpled, meaningless paper, trying to smile, his right hand in his pants-pocket while the torn bag followed his left hand to his mouth, a whole bag to hide what had once perhaps been a set of beautiful white teeth. Before all the apples heading toward the landing below had come to rest, he had already begun to pick up apples; he lost his big hat when he bent down toward the stone floor, had the apples in his hand, had to put them down again in order to grab the hat, began to gather them up again, in his pockets, in his hands, in his arms with his hands clasped and there were still a good many apples left.

But what helpfulness! Children and grown-ups both, they were all bringing him apples, laying them in the basket his arms made against his thick body; he moved to raise his hat in thanks, lost the apples again, tried to smile at his clumsiness with his lips pressed together – what a singular grimace – and finally the first word they heard him say: a pure old-fashioned Swedish *tack* – thanks, thanks, thanks for each apple, that little word thanks, so easy to say, so hard to say; how to say thanks I shall never forget, I say thanks at home, I say thanks as a guest. And then all the apples in his arms, every last apple, and all the apple-bringers, children and grown-ups, surrounding him, and the door right beside him, but how to get the keys out? Then in the same quick, slightly stumbling but correct Swedish: Help me – just for a second. And he transferred all the apples to the arms of the person standing nearest, got the keys out and the door barely open so no one could see in, then all the fruit back in his arms, then the broad of his back toward the assembly and his body in the opening of the door, and threw all the apples into the apartment, you could hear them thud and thud on the floor, then he turned around again face to face, passed his hand over his damp forehead and moved his fingers down as if cleaning the corners of his mouth, drew a breath as if he were preparing a speech. Extended his hand and pointed toward the narrow crack of the door. Flustered. And everyone waited. And the words almost a whisper and ashamed:

It's so ugly in there.

2

It was so ugly in there.

He stood staring into the two rooms without seeing, breathing heavily, an intense pain behind his forehead. He blanked out, everything dark and empty, where were his familiar five senses? Gradually, small angry red spots on his retinas; they were all the shiny apples that lay scattered across the floor. He came to himself slowly, very slowly. Now his hearing: he listened behind him, toward the door, quiet on the other side, they must have gone off, all the helpful ones, it must have happened during the seconds or minutes when he was oblivious, the short space of time which he would never be able to chart because his memory had been asleep, so it wasn't possible to get back there. That didn't matter, of course, but it was disturbing; he had to work to prevent anxiety from taking advantage of the small lacuna in consciousness.

He bent down and began gathering apples again, with a painful feeling of repetition and humiliation. He straightened up and surveyed the ugliness, no bowl, no large plate, not on the table, not on the shapeless old sideboard that had been ridiculously cheap and now was just ridiculous. Nothing but bags, and of course he'd had a bag to set among the other bags – the one with bread, the one with eggs, the one with the cheese that would soon be too old – that's where the one full of apples would have stood; now he had to lay them loose on the sideboard, it wasn't all that terrible, it wasn't all that terrible.

He started to mutter, he bustled about with his fine apples, muttering that it wasn't all that terrible, until he began to chuckle, the whole thing was really too absurd. He brought his hand to his mouth but took it down again, wasn't necessary here, he was alone after all, alone with the door closed, no one could take him by surprise. All at once he felt warm – no wonder, his hat and coat still on. He struggled out of the coat and laid it carefully over a chair with curved legs and upholstery of shabby red velvet – had no doubt been beautiful once. He put his hat on top, gave a tug to his vest, which was riding up his belly accordion-fashion, sat down in the leather armchair, his heavy hands slack on the armrests, and leaning back gently now, he wearily shut his eyes and sucked loudly on his brown stumps of teeth.

If only he had a cigar left; but he didn't. Had forgotten to buy one, maybe forgotten in order to economize, maybe just forgotten, didn't really know. Over in the ashtray, or what he called the ashtray, there was no stump; he knew that because he remembered turning the jar-lid upside down over the garbage pail before going out in the morning. And to go out and buy himself one now? No, mustn't move, couldn't bear that whole business of stairs and people yet again today, couldn't manage to behave himself and conduct himself, it was too complicated, too taxing. He sat motionless and felt the tension in his diaphragm, the dry sucking far back in his throat, everything he had to overcome now until some other need or requirement came along. Dusk fell, the darkness behind his eyelids thickened, he heard his breathing grow regular, drowsy, perhaps he was resting now, perhaps this was what you called resting.

He began to hum, far down in his throat and very quietly; his voice rasped and faltered, ugly, but it was just a prop for something he heard inside himself that sounded very beautiful, very pleasing. What was it? He sat guessing for a while, Mozart, Haydn? He smiled: Must be Haydn. Moved his head to the rhythm, the intervals felt like little tickling leaps in his throat. Music. Never heard music anymore, never went to a concert, didn't want to have a radio. Before. He could see himself in the concert halls, young, handsome, enthusiastic, truly an excellent listener. He could see himself during the intermissions, strolling confidently with the rest of the audience, two streams of voices and colors that met and passed each other, waiting for the signal, waiting for the sound of the instruments being tuned anew, the conductor, the soloist and then the music; it was so festive, so soothing, created such communion.

He opened his mouth and sang louder, his heavy lower lip quavered. That joyful motif like a fanfare over and over again – surely that was the cello concerto? And in fact the cello was the instrument his throat mimicked best, the deep, warm and reserved instrument, raspy in its attacks. He started to laugh, sounded as if the cellist's hand had begun to tremble so the bow skipped on the strings; here he sat, decayed old Silberstein, comparing himself to a cello – this noble instrument, as it's always so beautifully called – sat here and let the notes scratch the itch for tobacco that was tickling his throat, and became a cello set on a festively lit stage for reverence and admiration.

It was certainly comical, and he liked to see himself as comical, it supplied a familiar relief from bitterness and fear. He tried to hold onto the cello game, oh it was so absurd, decayed old Silberstein – he stretched one arm up as the instrument's neck and scratched himself on the belly with his other hand, really playing himself for the fool, now a powerful forte so his voice seized and he started to cough, folding up at the thought of the neighbors, their curiosity, surprise and perhaps disgust, and then his self-contempt suddenly broke out; the grotesque lost its comical veneer and became merely grotesque, ugly, loathsome. There he sat now hunched up over his coughing, leaning forward with his arms crossed over his swollen paunch and with saliva and phlegm in the corners of his mouth and everything had shifted very fast, everything was very painful, the memory of the ridiculous game and then all the days ahead that had to be lived as if under the sign of that silliness; it felt as if life had taken a new, bitter direction in that moment of embarrassing foolishness. He felt like this often and thought, It will pass, it always passes, I know it will pass, I know, yet he was still afraid that everything might get stuck, become final, and he wished they would come in and hit him and torment him, torture him on the level where he could tolerate himself, where the humiliation came from external force, and not from an internal lack of resistance.

They, they, they; which ones am I thinking of, he wondered, which ones are supposed to come in, which ones are supposed to hit and torment me. And he began to think of the faces here in the building, searching for the brutality that would exonerate him. And then at once he grew ashamed: here was evil lurking within him.

His own evil.

Evil. The word had a taste of naïveté, childhood. It was a word from long ago, from the time it was so tempting to remember as pure, uncomplicated, clear. He sighed. Felt very tired. The feeling of shame gnawed at him. He stood up and began to lumber back and forth in the apartment, his arms hung down, his head projected forward, his shoes seemed heavy. Stopped at the big, old sideboard, let his fingers stroke the worn mahogany surface, thought he was remembering something, tried to pin it down but it slid away, leaving behind only a fleeting color or taste. He opened the bread bag and dug into the soft bread, stuffed his mouth, chewed with difficulty, ground his jaws together stubbornly, lumbered off again. The bread swelled in his mouth, dry; eating it was slow going. He had hoped that he was hungry, but clearly he wasn't. He drank a little water, it smelled of chlorine, tasted of rust, but was cool, refreshing. The craving for tobacco rose up anew in him, persistent, urgent, but this time he almost liked it, the craving was just as numbing as the satisfaction. He worked it up on purpose, thought about big aromatic cigars and cool blue smoke, made up slogans for an advertising campaign, drew and puffed with a voluptuously pouted mouth.

But he knew that it couldn't last long. He mustn't intensify it until it was unbearable, mustn't tempt the discomfort out to where it missed its target and exploded all over him, over his thoughts, memories, over his whole being. He began searching for a new temptation, but found none, he was too tired, too exhausted, there wasn't much that could manage to arouse his resistance. He ought to clean up in here, of course, make sure it was clean, neat, pleasant. But it was just so hopelessly ugly, the whole place.

He stood in the middle of the floor and looked around. There was a lot to be done, too much. He stared at the two chests in the corner; he would have to get himself to ask if the apartment came with a storage space in the attic or the cellar. But first of course he had to unpack what was still in them, old repulsive saucepans, chipped crockery – obstinately he went over a dreary inventory in his head.

This was his property. This stuff was what he owned. And then that ridiculous business that was his, the small storeroom with all the pomades and ointments, the company called Chemprodukt, that musty hole where he passed his days trying to sell what he considered worthless, he could hear how his voice sounded on the telephone, flat, without confidence in himself, without faith in the products, that really wasn't how a good salesman sounded. And then every time the receiver rested silent in the cradle: the worry that he might have spent too much money; nothing was happening here, after all, no one phoned with orders, he just sat around crumpled up amid these embarrassing jars and tubes, all the stock that he'd gotten hold of at such a remarkably low price and that was to have given him the small profit he needed in order to exist.

To exist. How many people were supposed to eke out an existence from the jars? The manufacturer, he himself, and then all the barbers, hairdressers, druggists whom he bothered day in and day out with his viscous humility, and who had no more faith in the value of his products than he did but clearly took greater pleasure in business.

Greater pleasure in business. He smiled. All that was so oddly distant to him, an affliction far far away as soon as the door clattered shut and he climbed the seven steps up to the street. Everything that he could never see as enterprise, only as duress, necessity.

The gloomy storeroom, the gloomy apartment, the gloomy path between them. He smiled again. Everything was really reduced, to the utmost degree. He could be pleased. No one could envy him anything, he had nothing to lose, they could just as well take everything away from him. He went and sat in the chair they could just as well take away from him, this really very comfortable armchair that would be so easy to forget, he looked at the table, the sideboard, the bed, all these things that it would be so ridiculously easy to part from.

He began to feel quite cheerful. He abandoned himself to his sudden changes of mood, they made him feel vigorous, alive. He slapped his hands against the armrests. He got up, he thought perhaps he was hungry, he found a knife and started carving away at the cheese, it was a bit old but probably still good, no it wasn't, it tasted of mold, it was as if it tasted of the room, this too he could truly part from without any great regret.

He fumbled among the bags on the sideboard. It had grown dark. He took an egg, broke it at both ends and sucked it up raw, he didn't like it, but he often did this even though in some odd way it frightened him. Or perhaps precisely because of that. Tickle the fear a little, pay it tribute in small, carefully measured portions so it wouldn't feel moved to gather its strength for a proper attack.

And then an apple, which would have felt so fresh if he'd had sound teeth. Now more like a reminder of defects and disintegration, and a slight pain when the overly large pieces forced their way down his throat.

Suddenly he felt cold. He rubbed his palms together, it would have been good now to have a warm and comfortable smoking jacket. Smoke. Smoking jacket. Good to have. Had he come around to that again? The desire to have and acquire, the wish that so easily panicked him. Frightened, he stuffed his hands into the baggy pockets of his jacket, fingered loose change and crumbs of tobacco. Death. Annihilation. The oversensitive nerves in his worn-down teeth were directly hooked up to the brain cell that harbored his absurd fear of dying. The desire to own things was also connected there. Everything, everything tunneled into that cavity, he could never be left in peace, it was abominable.

He shook his head, he whimpered, he carried on, it was as if someone had gripped his arms and begun to twist, harder, harder, now something must finally give way and break. He threw himself onto the bed, he would get still more rumpled and disheveled but he didn't have the strength to get up, only to toss back and forth on the bed with his hands pressed against his rib cage as if to help draw the breaths that came so hard.

Try to think about people. Not the past, not the future, but people here, now, in this building. But he didn't even know what they looked like, almost never looked anyone in the face, had no idea of their character or their life that might help him make up gentle fantasies about community, appreciation, trust. And too, such fantasies were of course only ways of tempting yourself, of luring yourself toward the possibility of severe disappointments and excessive pain. No, better to imagine the faces with brutal grimaces, as he had a short while ago; then he thought he could recognize them and loneliness became a retreat, a course of action marked by good sense and careful consideration. He was surveying his life, controlling it, flight isn't always the humiliation of passivity.

These two rooms of his. This closed door of his. Just now this would have to do. Just now there wasn't anything else, perhaps. It was a game that he often played. Calmed him sometimes. But why then this tight feeling across his chest? Must he always long for something else?

Be forced to come up with new games? But he was worn out, couldn't do it anymore; his inventiveness, his imagination, his mastery – they were all so exhausted. This place was his last stop. It was perhaps in these rooms that in the end he would die. Behind this closed door. How long would it take before someone broke in to see what was wrong? Until the soursweet smell of corpse seeped out into the hall. For there was in fact no one, no one. Self-pity. There were only unknown faces streaming in, filling the doorway, whispering in the hall. Only disgust on them. And then one of the practical and enterprising types, someone truly self-important, a few brief phone calls and it would all be over. And very quickly forgotten.

He began at last to feel sleepy. It was so enormously welcome; he just had to dig himself out of these baggy old clothes and nestle in under the dirty cover. The deadening hum somewhere inside his head would grow and eventually cover the whole world. Nothing would be left but a steady and distant rushing sound.

He got up with difficulty. His legs wobbled under him. So tired. He tottered over to the window. Now that it was dark outside the dirt on the panes couldn't trouble him. For the first time all evening he looked out. He leaned heavily against the windowsill, looked down, the few streetlights were far apart, it was very empty out there. He raised his head, it was so heavy; he looked upwards. The sky was completely clear, he saw the stars, all those other worlds, everything that must be inconceivably different, and for a moment a feeling of loss came over him because he was no longer capable of crying.

3

A crooked, embarrassed smile to his reflection, the same as every morning. Opened wide as he slid the razor over his cheeks, had to pull the slack skin tight, nonetheless there were always small cuts for the styptic pencil. His hollow mouth, much too red. His heavy eyelids, the night still apparent in their swelling, these days cold water couldn't heal as it used to. Now it took coffee and something to smoke too; coffee he had, it was in a bag in a drawer in the sideboard in the room in the building in the city in the country where he lived, but it would still be a couple of hours before the tobacco shops opened, he would have to put up with the red swelling in his face, the swelling that was not at all due to tears, only to limp fatigue. How loosely his hand held the old-fashioned razor with the engraved name; he'd gotten it ages ago from his mama Mutti mother mère; Emanuel, it said in elegant letters, and that means God is with us.

Now we'll be careful, he said, his voice hoarse and warm from sleep, now we'll be careful because your hand is shaky and the blade dull and all the little children spit as you go by.

He grimaced even more.

All the little children, he said, all the little children, you love to talk like old ballads, and your old ballads are all too often nasty about others and nice to you, and you forget that God loves the little children no matter how obnoxious they are – and his love doesn't burn out until they've turned seventeen, even though it's begun to cool off by the time they reach twelve.

He put the razor away.

He filled the basin, bent over and plunged his face into the cold water – so wonderfully refreshing it was out of place here. He snorted, rubbed away lather and bits of skin, then saw in the mirror how the water was streaming along folds and wrinkles, that's how I look with tears down my cheeks – *uff!*

And now "with rosy cheek and sunny gaze," he said aloud and laughed – *double uff!* He chuckled. When a face gets worn out it's not good for anything, all expressions become grotesque, just keep it straight and let it shine with all your experience, then they can come and talk about the wisdom and resignation of old age. A sham! it's only your face going on strike, and my face aged very early. You're born with a little wrinkled mug like an old geezer's, then there are a few years when it lends itself to beauty and human passions and gets called the mirror of the soul, and then you're in a mask again with your range of expressions cut back and your soul is fluttering behind a stiffened monument, a tired old insect gone astray and buzzing against the dirty windowpane. So helpless.

Where are you, Mammi?

How lucky that she's gone. Mammi – I have no lips for that word anymore.

Papsi, then?

He chuckled. Lucky that everyone was gone, that everything was empty and lost, that this face had no occasion to turn to any person who concerned him in any way, that no one would search for reactions, feelings and messages in the ugly, wrinkled mask. He turned his face away from the mirror, felt the smarting from all the thousands of small wounds left by the razor, both the visible and the invisible ones.

It still hurts, he said; it still hurts.

He got dressed, his clothes were sackcloth and he himself was ashes. He brewed coffee, strong and bitter. He drank it very slowly, slurping it, for a few restful moments he imagined his brain was completely empty, only his throat and stomach existed, and they existed only to receive the good, warm coffee.

I have no worries, he thought next, and first it was a comfortable, then an uncomfortable, then a painful thought. I have no worries. It was so naked, as naked as he'd always wanted it to be – to rest in the dead absence of worry.

I'm always coming back to that one.

You're always coming back to that one.

He's always coming back to that one.

First I, then you, then he. The nice little game of putting yourself at arm's length with the help of the pronouns; could be used to advantage in times of temptation.

What is it he's always coming back to?

Whether he should dare to let loose the spark that's glinting deep inside the ashes; this is the temptation.

I: yes. . . . You: maybe. He: no!

Conquered.

For the moment it's conquered.

I have no worries is a good and comfortable thought again.

And the cup's empty and it's time for a refill. Intensely aware of every movement and every sound, he poured out more coffee for himself, he did it well, got so taken up with the little ritual that there wasn't room for anything else in his head. He added sugar, stirred with the spoon, drank. Everything was wonderfully important, everything that was wonderfully insignificant.

How are you making out these days, Emanuel?

I'm just fine thanks, Mammi.

Lots of friends, like before, Emanuel?

No, Mammi, I'm just fine.

Some girlfriends then? Maybe you'll get married, have a wife and children?

No, Mammi, I'm just fine.

I'd so like to have some grandchildren, Emanuel, I like children so much, you were so beautiful when you were little, always played so nicely, hardly ever cried, were so easy to take care of.

Now I'm smiling at you, Mammi. Laughing, almost.

How's business, Emanuel?

Fine thanks, Papsi, I'm earning next to nothing, I own some worthless pomades, I'm very satisfied with my situation.

We Silbersteins . . .

Yes yes, Papsi, I know, we have always been ambitious and hard-working, no matter where we've been we have created employment, money, we have produced, we have been a joy to ourselves and others, I know, I know.

You mustn't mock. . . .

But I'm not mocking, Papsi, absolutely not. Look at me. I'm rubbing my brow, I'm confused, I'm stammering, I don't know how to answer you. I sit here thinking about all your industriousness, I truly don't know how I can answer you.

One has to keep trying . . .

No, Papsi, you're wrong there, you mustn't have such limitless faith in people.

Now you're being cynical, Emanuel.

No, I'm a realist, judge the possibilities according to the givens, of which I myself am the most essential. One could perhaps say that I am damaged.

Haven't we Silbersteins, countless times . . .

Exactly, Papsi. Far too many times.

He sighed, troubled. Got up, went over to the dirty window. The street. The day was starting to show itself down there. Traffic, people. He wished the apartment faced the back yard, the empty lot. That would have suited him better. Such a small apartment should be at the back. This house was strange – built wrong. It was only right that it should be torn down. It was good that it would disappear, be obliterated, forgotten. It was ugly and stupid. The front should always have grand, spacious apartments. Façades should exhibit wealth, contentedness, confidence. Buildings shouldn't put their failures on display. His life was a backyard existence.

He got angry. He felt exposed, ridiculed. Why couldn't he be left in peace? It seemed to him that people down there were eyeing his unwashed windows. What gall. He clenched his fists deep in the baggy pockets of his jacket. He began to mumble, shifted his weight from one foot to the other, swayed like an old bear. He was playing the fool, he knew why perfectly well: he had to work himself up a bit to be able to go out. This was his usual morning exercise.

You've become altogether too solitary, Emanuel.

You can say that, Sara, because you never had time to get old, never really had a chance to grasp . . .

Will you stand still, Emanuel!

You got to die, Sara, you never reached . . .

You mustn't be so bitter, Emanuel.

But I'm not bitter, Sara. I'm satisfied. I lead a livable life, I want it this way, I've gotten used to it.

A laughable life.

A livable life, I said, dear sister. You can't understand how absurd everything's become, you never got to live through the really frightening parts.

I . . .

I don't want to talk with you about this, Sara. I'm so glad that you were spared the whole thing and I don't want to talk with you about it. I know I've gotten very ugly, very difficult; I have to go earn my living now, I wish you wouldn't keep me, it's hard enough as it is.

There – you see?

Yes I know I'm disjointed, but you can't expect anything else of human beings, can you.

You say that you're satisfied.

Spare me having to mull it over. Satisfied or not satisfied, it's all the same to me, Sara.

All right, get going, then.

Well, there's no great hurry, after all. Besides, I can do without tobacco for a little while yet.

But you said it was work . . .

It's my craving for a smoke that's going to help me get out there, dear Sara. Life's grim necessities for a debilitated old Jew.

He tittered and chuckled. He was really good at repartee. In a way she was right: he was too solitary, it made him eccentric and he couldn't afford to be eccentric. He had to behave naturally, with natural dignity; deviations were risky. Being solitary was both protection and danger – oh, how heavy and impossible it all was. He had become unskilled at living – we who are so well known for our skill at that, he thought. And where have all our abilities gotten us? But he was probably an oddity, he couldn't tell, he had no contact with the others anymore, after all; the clan instinct is dangerous, causes bad blood. They say we stick together, and it's always reproach, criticism. We stuck together during the war – that's fine to say about anyone else, but not us. We didn't stick together during the war – that's not all right to say either, nothing is all right to say, the point is to make sure that nothing at all gets said.

Go ahead and despise me, Papsi!

But I'm telling you that I'm damaged, that I'm ruined, I can blame it on anything you like, you'll see, in that department my ingenuity knows no bounds.

Papsi, Papsi, it sounds wonderfully grotesque, I'm glad we had this wonderfully grotesque pet name for you, I repeat it to myself until I laugh and you disappear, I puff you out like a little cloud of smoke through my big nose, away with you, away with the whole lot of you!

He waved his arms, gesticulated, danced. Day after day this clumsy war dance in this ugly, cramped apartment: truly – truly a very bizarre life; really – really very different from the one he'd imagined once. But what he'd once imagined was now as remote, as absurdly alien, as if it had been thought of by a completely different person, and that was really the case, after all. Nothing – neither body nor soul – bore the slightest resemblance to this cavorting buffoon; where were the books, the music, the families, the prospering businesses, the close friends, the good people, the little dark-eyed girlfriends, everything his heart and his body could have taken as an altogether natural framework for life? The same heart, the same body as now? Not a chance.

The beautiful wallpaper, the beautiful pictures, the beautiful furniture, the beautiful china, the beautiful silver, that was really the dumbest film he could crank through his head. He didn't want to see it – it was just dumb and trivial, a little bit ridiculous, a dated work of art.

And these ridiculous old gentlemen who moved around in these ridiculous salons smoking ridiculously big cigars and speaking of religion and culture as significant phenomena – it was all a farce, a crude and poorly done farce.

About that much I'm surely right, he said out loud, angrily, and even if I'm not right then I have the right to feel and think that way, and if I don't have that right then I'll take it, and I won't long for the past, no one's going to get me to admit that I long for the past, and if I do then it's only temporary indisposition, sickness, it's only sickness.

Again this artificial anger as a little nudge toward the door. It was really time to get going, just a question of getting in the mood for the difficult trial. He searched for his anger and his craving for tobacco, all the forces of good had to be mobilized. He picked up his overcoat, it was in miserable condition – excellent: something he could really swear about. The same with his hat – it was supposed to be black, was looking more and more like shitty gray, the clever bastard who'd succeeded in selling it was no mediocre businessman, now there was a person he could learn something from, he should certainly keep him in mind when he was dithering in his rat-hole and answering "why, yes" to every dumb question about quality and suitability. My jars at my prices are an outright donation to mankind, a pure and beautiful gift, don't miss it, don't miss it! Turn and stare when I go scampering through the streets, you're looking at one of mankind's benefactors, smell that good sweet fragrance from your fellowman's sleek and silky skull and be thankful to me, for there you have my great and lasting contribution to the wonderful society I have been granted the inconceivable good fortune to live in!

With his overcoat and hat on he rushed around the apartment doing something he imagined was tidying up: he smoothed out the bed, dumped the grounds out of the coffee pot, sloshed water in the cup, rustled a few bags, wiped his bare hand across the windowsill, rinsed it off in the sink. He was just procrastinating, he began moving chairs, rearranged the furniture – much nicer this way, would make it so much easier to come home, in fact it would be good to come home to this new and fresh-looking apartment.

He was panting, he'd done it all too fast, he came to a stop and straightened his back, it hurt a little; then a few uncertain steps into the vestibule, turned the switch on and turned it off, the light was working – excellent.

Then a few steps more, now he was standing in front of the door. Had he forgotten anything? Of course not, and he hadn't thought so, either. There was no way to postpone it any longer. He thrust his hand deep into his pants pocket. Yes, the keys were where they should be. He raised his hand slowly toward the lock, but started violently.

His doorbell was ringing.

4

He stood completely still, tried to think, tried to think clearly, he inhaled deeply, tried to make his breathing calm, regular. This can't be anything, he tried to tell himself, that can in any way be dangerous, unpleasant or painful. But at the same time his hand started to tremble, he'd forgotten it in midair, it was still stretched out toward the lock, slowly he withdrew it, hid it foolishly behind his back like a child. I don't have to open up, after all, he tried to tell himself. I can do exactly as I please, I can open up or not open up, that's something I decide completely on my own. At the same time: decide, I don't want to decide, I want to be left in peace. And of course he had a right to be left alone, really had a right to it, the law gave him that right and it was the law that counted, at least until it stopped counting, until people set themselves above it and it got rewritten and changed because people set themselves above the law and it was no longer popular for him to have the right to be left in peace. But that's just how he mustn't think, he had to trust in his door, and he had behaved, after all, in such a way that he should have been able to trust in his door, but then you never knew, because strictly speaking it didn't have a thing to do with how he behaved, one fine day they broke the door down anyway, and that's when he'd laugh at them, because of course they'd only find an old Jew diminished in every way and a household that was so ugly and worthless that it wouldn't even be fun to smash up.

The doorbell rang again.

And if he opened up? As long as they were ringing at the door, not kicking it, not banging on it and shouting, then he could still believe in their respect and goodwill, and maybe it was just a question of not trying their patience too long, maybe all he needed to do to satisfy them was open the door, bow, and smile in a friendly way, maybe their mission was just to see him bow. In that case it really was important not to delay too long, perhaps too much time had passed already, he had to come up with reasons and excuses, but it was of course just that sort of thing he couldn't manage anymore, his imagination was miserably slow these days. And the seconds going by and he was standing here as if paralyzed. He still hadn't made a movement that they could have perceived on the other side of the door, perhaps he could still choose between being home and not being home. But maybe they'd heard his labored breathing, like sighs to sneer at out there in the stairwell, or had they perhaps . . .

No, he had been extremely alert the whole time and he hadn't heard any steps, they certainly hadn't gone away. But if they'd sneaked off . . . Were already someplace far from here and roaring with laughter, knowing that he was standing here like a statue and staring at the ugly door. In that case they could go right ahead and laugh, just so they'd gone, he'd been ridiculous for a long time already, it didn't bother him anymore, dignity was an old outmoded decoration for secure officials in drowsy welfare states. Drowsy . . . it was he himself who was suddenly drowsy, what a surprise, he could never understand it, a whole life and he could still amaze himself, he needed to yawn, had no doubt gotten too little oxygen when he tried to breathe so no one could hear him, and now he was standing here facing a closed door with his mouth wide open.

Shut your mouth and open the door, that's the only thing to do.

He opened the door.

How grotesque!

A gray old lady with a smile as crooked as his own, who nodded as politely as he bowed.

More embarrassed than curious as she faced the narrow slit, the door as usual less than half open.

Sorry, she said, I rang at the wrong door.

Twice!

Yes I rang at the wrong door.

Whom were you looking for?

No one. I live in the building.

Do you ring at your own door?

No, no, just happened to touch your bell, Mr. Silberstein, it was a mistake, I didn't mean to ring at all.

But twice!

Oh the second time just to say I was sorry, Mr. Silberstein. It was such a nuisance, after all, such an utter nuisance.

By all means.

My name is Miss Svensson – Librarian Svensson – I live here in the building, I happened to touch your doorbell – on my way out – on my way to the library where I work. I live here in the building. You might say that we're neighbors.

Indeed.

Neighbors. To be neighbors. Before it used to mean something, a kind of connection, you might say, but nowadays – don't you agree, Mr. Silberstein.

Absolutely.

I think it's so crazy, somehow warped and hostile to life.

It's as it should be.

You can think so if you like, Mr. Silberstein. Neighbors, such a beautiful word with an old ring to it, would be a terrible shame if it lost its meaning. But here I am, chatting away.

I suppose you've got to hurry off to the library.

No, not in the least, we needn't hurry on my account, Mr. Silberstein. But you. I see you have your coat on, your hat on your head . . .

Pardon me!

Of course – it wasn't a criticism, Mr. Silberstein, I just mean that I'm keeping you.

Yes, I was about to . . .

I understand perfectly, Mr. Silberstein. Oh, I just happened to touch your doorbell . . .

Twice, and the second time to say you were sorry.

Exactly, you mustn't be annoyed with me, Mr. Silberstein. I'm a trifle embarrassed about the blunder and one has to be patient in one's dealings with people. You seem so isolated to me. Perhaps a misanthropic streak.

I have a misanthropic streak.

I understand perfectly, Mr. Silberstein, after everything that you've had to go through.

Go through?

Oh, I understand perfectly, Mr. Silberstein, you're finding me intrusive now, but I'm not going to . . .

No, you're not.

Of course not, but I've always felt you were so congenial, Mr. Silberstein.

Always. I've lived here a very short time.

But one gets a certain impression of people, I credit myself with having a certain sense . . .

I'm sure.

And here I am treading water and not getting on my way. It's almost starting to get a bit comical.

Very.

You're so curt with me, Mr. Silberstein. I understand very well that you mistrust people.

I certainly don't mean to be unfriendly . . .

No – oh, I understand so well! But your fate . . .

My fate?

Oh yes, there are so many frightful things going on nowadays. But one mustn't despair of people.

Of course not.

I'm so glad that you agree with me about that, Mr. Silberstein. That even a person with your past can still trust.

My past?

Yes, exactly, Mr. Silberstein. In my life, I've been so comfortable . . . But we weren't going to speak about me, after all.

We were going to go to our jobs.

To be sure, you to yours, I to mine. That's how life is. Imagine if people were a little better at meeting each other, if we could really meet each other, I mean.

The endless stream of words suddenly stopped, it was quiet, they stood staring foolishly at each other. Have I been too unfriendly now, he thought, or have I perhaps been too friendly. Have I offended her, so that she'll spread slander about me in the building, or have I let her get too close to me. Of all things, conversation and words are the riskiest, but how can you evade. It's not just a question of your own words, after all, but of the others', even my silence becomes an insult or a kindness, I can't. . . .

And as, ridiculously, they held their positions in the embarrassing lull, he began to feel warm inside his overcoat. He had to get going now, but of course she was blocking the narrow opening of the door with her disgustingly well-meaning person.

Suddenly, without really knowing how it had happened, he had slammed the door shut with a bang that echoed in the stairwell, brutally and inconsiderately he left her alone in their dead end. He knew that now he must have insulted her, it was a relief, he thought finally he knew where they stood, finally there was an enemy, someone he could focus on in his fantasies about the dangers that this apparently peaceful apartment building held in store. He could picture her already, rushing in and out of the various apartments, full of horror at his atrocious, yes dangerous behavior, oh what she hadn't been subjected to, she who had approached him with so much friendliness and understanding, the man was dangerous, probably criminal, his shadiness, his taciturnity, his careful sneaking in and out, what did he have in that apartment that no one ever got a glimpse into and whose door was never opened more than a crack?

Suddenly he heard a cautious scratching at the door, like a dog that wants to be let in. Then silence again, and then surprisingly light footsteps on the stairs, going down. The library will be opening soon now, he thought, they'll have lots to say about newcomers there today. But I'm no newcomer, after all, so of course it can't be about me, I can safely go to what I call my job.

Carefully, he opened the door slightly, there was no one out there, now the thing was to get going fast. He quickly shut the door behind him, and now the heavy loping down the stairs. The whole stairwell was empty, unusual for the morning, but then, he was late. This time of day was evidently excellent for setting out, it went smoothly, was easy, the stress was negligible. He became almost cheerful. Now there was only the entrance door left, then he would be out on the street and at once it would be a different story, he wasn't recognized there, seldom needed to hesitate about whether or not to greet someone, there were different routes, different sidewalks to choose from. So out the door we go!

There she stood on the other side of the street, waiting – the librarian, Miss Svensson; smiling heartily she hurried across the roadway toward him, no chance of getting away.

I just want to apologize, she said.

Once more.

You must have found me unbearable, and very gauche besides, very unladylike.

Not at all.

Oh yes, I understand very well, you want nothing but to be left in peace, do you.

No.

And I . . . Can you forgive me?

I seem to recall that I've already done so.

You're taking the liberty of joking a bit with me, Mr. Silberstein, yes indeed, of downright poking a little fun at me, that strikes me as a good sign, indicates a certain contact, playful perhaps, but contact?

Why should we make contact?

But, Mr. Silberstein! Surely one can't deny the deep value of human contact. Contact between people – is there anything more beautiful, anything more important. I think that a great many of the world's and people's troubles are caused by inadequate contact. Can't you share my view, Mr. Silberstein?

No.

But . . .

No one can share anyone else's view.

But Mr. Silberstein!

That's my view. I don't ask you to share it.

Now you're being very clever, Mr. Silberstein.

That wasn't my intention.

She smiled her crooked smile at him, remained standing there, he was still in her grasp. Old hand at conversation, he thought, I am a conversationalist from way back, but for this conversation I can't come up with an ending.

I'm afraid I've got to be going now.

Which way, Mr. Silberstein?

My way.

A trifle discourteous, Mr. Silberstein. But I understand so perfectly . . .

Well, then.

And then underway. Slightly faster than he could manage. As usual. Didn't turn around. Didn't want to see her expression. Didn't want to see if she was following him. Didn't want to think about her. Just think ahead, a very short way ahead, just to the miserable hole of a cellar with the stupid jars, and not even that far at first, think one block and one streetcorner ahead at a time. Let your mind follow your feet and your body. Keep a firm grip on your mind, don't let it get even one meter ahead of you. Force it to trot obediently and stupidly alongside you.

He could take slower steps now.

If worst comes to worst, you make the steps themselves help you. You count them. That can be a useful trick. Or you observe very precisely where you put your feet down.

Or you let your mind run ahead ten-twelve meters. To the next lamppost, for example. Let it wait there. Overtake it, quick and by surprise or slowly, teasing it.

The mind offers endless possibilities.

That's what they say, after all.

Again this grotesque giggling that made people turn around, shake their heads, sneer or get annoyed.

He quickened his pace again.

A lurching race through the streets.

Then: one turn of a corner and two cross-streets remaining now before the hole in the cellar. Two cross-streets. One cross-street. Right over there.

Right.

There.

The steps. The door. The light. It was so dim here, always a wearisome gloom. The table with the silent, waiting telephone.

He sat down heavily. Laid the long list of telephone numbers neatly in front of him. Got up again. Took off coat and hat and threw them on a crate. Sat there again. Looked at his watch. Time to start. Really time to start.

But the morning's conversation with Miss Svensson remained in him as a residue of embarrassment and discomfort.

How ridiculous.

He saw before him her expectant face. He heard her ingratiatingly friendly voice.

She was horrible and meddlesome.

He tried to laugh at her to be rid of her, but the laugh sounded sick and off-target here in the solitude of pomades.

Abominable not to be left in peace.

He missed her.

5

No, said Renkvist, no, I don't like them. I do not, and it's because you're supposed to like them. You have to like them because otherwise you feel you're being an anti-Semite. And you don't want to be an anti-Semite. But you don't like people that you have to like because it's nasty not to like them.

He laughed.

I'm an anti-Semite, then, because I don't want to be one.

He laughed again.

Take this ugly old Jew that's moved into the building, for example. I have to suppress the least little quiver of unpleasantness I feel around him because I'm so afraid of being an anti-Semite. But after all, even the people you like the most give you unpleasant feelings now and then. There's nothing strange or particularly troubling about that. But these people – we've got it into our heads that we have to love them at all times and at all costs. No damn wonder they're disliked.

Exactly the way those Jesus-people who feel they have to love their neighbors get so exceptionally malicious and intolerant.

Exaggeration, said Mrs. Renkvist.

Sure, said Renkvist, but if you don't exaggerate when you're clarifying the concepts, you end up with no concepts.

Why clarify the concepts, then, asked Mrs. Renkvist.

That I can answer, so you missed the mark this time, said Renkvist. In order to get one's hideous anti-Semitism under control.

Why do that, then?

Easy for you to say, since you don't have a damn drop of anti-Semitism in you.

Hardly know any Jews.

Now what on earth does that have to do with it, said Renkvist.

He slurped his coffee, feeling sensible and pleased, scratched his ear, shifted his pack of cigarettes from his left jacket pocket to his right, smiled at his wife, picked his nose, reached for the newspaper, left it where it was.

Haven't you noticed, he continued, with what relief those quarter- and eighth-part Jews tell you about the slight impurity of their blood. Then they can disparage Jews to their heart's content without being suspect. All the hysterical Judeophiles smile in admiration and talk about self-criticism and ironic self-deprecation. Less hysterical people think it's tedious to listen to and then feel like they're being unsympathetic, or crypto-Nazi.

Exaggeration, said Mrs. Renkvist.

Let me exaggerate some more, said Renkvist, it clears the air. Ever since the old Jew moved in I've felt a need to clear the air.

But my dear –

Now you're upset, huh? I guess it was an awful thing to say. Even though it was well meant.

Was it an awful thing to say, asked Mrs. Renkvist.

Well, what on earth do you want from me, then? I say that the air needs to be cleared when an old Jew moves in and you don't think it's an awful thing to say. Do I have to say that he eats babies before your coffee will go down the wrong way.

But you didn't mean the air around him, after all, you meant the air around you. That's a wonderful idea. I'm waiting eagerly for a breath of fresh air.

I see, said Renkvist – which means that you're tired of the conversation. You get tired fast these days. You're running out of devotion.

He laughed.

Don't be too sure of yourself, said Mrs. Renkvist.

I'm not sure, said Renkvist. Never. Never by any means. That's probably why I'm such a lousy journalist.

Stop right there, said Mrs. Renkvist.

Oh yes, said Renkvist, if you measure me against my talents and my opportunities, then I'm a lousy journalist. I'm too uncertain. Aren't you going to object again?

Am I supposed to, asked Mrs. Renkvist.

It's your simple duty as a wife, said Renkvist. I'm being facetious but I'm angry. Really. But it's the fault of these Jews, after all, so I shouldn't take it out on you too much.

That you're not doing yourself proud as a journalist?

If it were only so. To have such a fine motive for one's ugly feelings. And such a good reason for one's half-failures. But those bogeymen never do me any harm and never have. Even the first one I met, in school, was an expert at losing aggies to everyone at recess – naturally so he wouldn't be called an aggie-jew.* Even that much he had to begrudge a thirsting instinctual anti-Semite.

Instinctual anti-Semite!

Shut up since you don't have any instincts, said Renkvist, and let me get my feelings off my heaving chest.

No, said Mrs. Renkvist. I don't care for this. You're harping. That's not good.

I'm harping, said Renkvist as he got up, because you don't want to understand what I'm talking about.

I understand very well what you're talking about, said Mrs. Renkvist, but not why you're talking about it so much.

I don't like being tested, said Renkvist. The old Jew is testing me. I don't like disliking him.

Why should you like or dislike? You don't even know him.

Why should I feel anything at all? Good Lord! I don't feel because I should or I want to, but because I do. Now don't say "Well stop feeling it, then"; I don't want any damned stupid and hard-hearted advice like that.

What should I say, in that case? You'd better tell me so I don't go wrong.

Now you're offended, said Renkvist. You see what he's up to. Well, I'm amusing at any rate, aren't I?

Yes, sure.

But you didn't laugh, did you? Why don't you laugh if I'm amusing?

To be honest, I think you're being disagreeable now, said Mrs. Renkvist. That's why I'm not laughing. It's rather unpleasant.

But of course that's what I think too. So help me out, why don't you. Either say something so beautiful about the old Jew

Kuljude, "marble-jew," a slang term for a boy who plays marbles too cautiously and is therefore seen as miserly. – R. G.

that I'll be able to shed voluptuous tears, or say something so bad about him that I'll be able to feel voluptuous contempt.

I don't want to talk about him at all.

Why not?

Because I don't know him.

So what! You're not usually so scrupulous about that. Why should he enjoy such privileges?

Am I supposed to get angry now?

Go right ahead, said Renkvist, as long as you answer. Why such scruples about the old Jew? Why suddenly so unnaturally objective and fair?

It's your fault.

My fault?

When you fall into a fit of emotion I try to be rational. And when you start raving about instincts I have to speak up for intellect.

That's topsy-turvy, of course, said Renkvist. Man is the rational creature, woman the instinctual.

Don't laugh it off now, said Mrs. Renkvist.

Yes, said Renkvist, yes I'll do that. I'll laugh it off. That would be nice. If I could come up with a really good joke right now it would be one hell of a relief.

Then we won't discuss the matter any further, said Mrs. Renkvist.

Now it's definitely you who feel relieved, said Renkvist. That's curious. I had no idea this subject made you uncomfortable.

It doesn't, said Mrs. Renkvist. It's you who make me uncomfortable. You want to waltz your way out of danger, but it's a pretty half-hearted waltz. You're flaunting your anti-Semitism the way the quarter-Jew flaunts his Jewish blood. You pretend you're ashamed, but you're not ashamed one bit.

So I should be ashamed too!

You certainly should, said Mrs. Renkvist calmly. Not of your anti-Semitism, because I don't think that would give the Jews a drop of satisfaction, but of your flaunting.

Be ashamed, said Renkvist. Ashamed! Female tactics! Female psychology!

Why should you rant about females when you don't even mean it?

To be unpleasant. That old Jew makes me need to be unpleasant. I don't want to feel I have the advantage of pleasantness over him. You see, it's all his fault. And then you have to feel obliged to like him.

Who ever put it into your head that you're obliged to like him?

That's the other side of the other side of the coin when it comes to racism and contempt for whole groups and discrimination of all kinds. You get so damned humane it's almost scary. You end up with a pathos without enough weight under it. Because your feelings don't hang in there with you on the curves. And then you get mad. Often at exactly the people who were supposed to benefit from your lovely pathos. Mad at them because they're the focus of the most difficult emotional demands. I guess it's a merry-go-round – funny.

Very.

I can hear that you don't believe it.

It's too elegant.

Elegant, said Renkvist. These days a person's not even allowed to formulate things well. Best to keep your trap shut.

He dug out a cigarette and lit up, smoked with slightly studied vehement puffs, avoided looking at her as she sat there sloshing her coffee in the cup and looking a trifle sad. Her glasses had a tendency to slip down her nose, it made her look ridiculous and it irritated him.

You don't think for a minute that one ought to try to figure out why one dislikes people, he said. *What* one dislikes is easy to see, but *why* is a harder question.

Now you mean me, said Mrs. Renkvist, finally putting the cup to her mouth.

What do you mean, said Renkvist, sounding guilty, that's

damned egocentric. We're talking here about people and ideas and large problems and pressing issues.

How's the self-examination coming along, then, she asked. Is it over now?

He fell silent for a moment.

Then he said, I don't like it when you disapprove of me.

I thought that was what you wanted me to do, said Mrs. Renkvist. And I don't like it when you want me to do that.

He sat down next to her at the table. She looked lonely and not at all happy.

Maybe I wanted to quarrel a little, he said in a conciliatory way. Why I don't know. Biological causes, I suppose. Good God, I'm beginning to get middle-aged and have morning temper.

And so you want to quarrel with me, said Mrs. Renkvist, because I irritate you. But why bring in what you call ideas and pressing issues . . .

I said that in jest, Renkvist said, jest and gibberish.

But why make use of that poor old Jew?

Why "poor," said Renkvist. How the hell do you know you should feel sorry for him?

I feel sorry for him because you're using him as a weapon against me.

But of course, he doesn't know about that, said Renkvist. So he can't very well suffer on account of it.

But one can imagine, said Mrs. Renkvist, that lots of people use him that way, and in that case he's to be pitied.

Let me think now, said Renkvist.

Gladly.

I have to reflect on whether what you've said is worth considering. At the very least, it certainly doesn't seem suspect on grounds of elegance. On the contrary – reassuringly clumsy. That poor weapon Mr. Silberstein!

Are you being ironic?

I don't know, said Renkvist. I don't think so. I'm being reflective as hell. That must mean my ill humor is easing up. The coffee gets my biology going and the Jews aren't quite so unsavory anymore. Though I still don't like them. But if I have something good for lunch maybe that'll pass too.

He smiled at her, but she didn't respond to his smile. She stayed serious and picked absently at the breadbasket.

Life must appear very capricious to people who are really exposed to it, she said. Mr. Silberstein must always see everything as pure chance.

Don't you, asked Renkvist.

Yes, sure, but I don't always experience it that way. I think I know it, but I very seldom have to confront that knowledge. Mr. Silberstein probably has it right in front of him all the time.

Are you curious about him?

Beginning to be. And that's your fault. Your cheerful blustering.

I'm sure he's grateful for any interest taken in him, said Renkvist.

You think so, she asked. I don't think so. There are too many people with a warped interest in him.

Every kind of interest is received with gratitude, said Renkvist; in that respect surely everyone's the same. It can be as warped and twisted as you please. Give him a year in the void and he'll probably be glad to get whatever's offered, no matter how slight the interest is or who it comes from – even if it's from a confirmed anti-Semite like yours truly.

Said Renkvist.

. . . quite simply because nihil humani a me alienum sit. . . .

Schoolmaster Olausson paused for effect and registered the question marks on all the impressed faces.

. . . or, nothing human must be alien to me, to put it in good Swedish. Mankind's behavior patterns in various situations and conflicts have always been objects of my interest and study. An indulgent exactitude, a benevolent objectivity, is what I wish to make my hallmark in the course of these studies. To call my detached interest in this Silberstein "morbid curiosity" therefore seems to me to be ridiculous.

He blew his nose hard and angrily into an uncommonly large handkerchief.

Moreover, I think the expression morbid curiosity has a distasteful, moralizing flavor and I think it's about time for us to rise above all meaningless moralizings and value judgments. If one has even passing acquaintance with the great Hägerström, then . . . well, on second thought perhaps I'll approach it on a simpler level.

He was in a better mood already.

I would, then, call my interest healthy, human and legitimate.

Without thereby implying any value judgments, he added for safety's sake.

As far as the Jews as a group are concerned, we do in fact find something that's called group psychology, which can be considered empirically grounded and not just loose metaphysics.

And now there was triumph in his voice.

Schoolmaster Olausson was completely alone in his apartment. Unfortunately, unfortunately. So many people would have derived both benefit and enjoyment from hearing all these good arguments, just as all the stupid or insolent objections he so calmly and elegantly refuted would have aroused their justified mirth.

To confound scientifically based observations of group psychology with prejudices seems to me to be a rather simple trick of demagoguery.

Pause. The truth took root in the imaginary listeners' simple souls. A pause learned in a course on public speaking and the art of self-presentation.

To put it mildly, said Olausson.

He paced back and forth across the floor for a moment, then remembered that one shouldn't do that, stopped: feet spread apart, stand firm, look your audience in the eyes, one at a time (how else?), give a feeling of personal contact with the lecturer.

Common ancestry, common religion, common interests et cetera constitute a group, and the members of it gradually come to exhibit certain common traits of character. There is no reason why the Jews should be an exception to this rule.

Silberstein belongs to this group.

He interests me partly as individual, partly as representative of this group.

Yes I know that by now many of you regard my presentation as suffering from a certain dryness, but these are points which I consider it necessary to establish. Even at the risk of not being thought sufficiently entertaining.

He grew irritated again, he sensed that he had gotten stuck.

Those who are not interested can leave, he said suddenly.

He observed with satisfaction that they all stayed, even though he had paused for a reasonable length of time to give each and every one of them a chance to depart.

This Silberstein, he continued, dissociates himself from the rest of us through his behavior – exclusive behavior, one might call it. By the rest of us I mean for example those who live in the building, or if we broaden the perspective, those who live in this city, and further, in the broadest sense, those who make their home in this country of ours. Even this exclusive behavior alone indicates that he regards himself as belonging to another group, another community.

And what harm does he do by that?

Suddenly he had posed a rhetorical question that he found a bit difficult to answer.

Quiet over there! he shouted.

It can in itself only be considered less than good, he continued, to place oneself outside that community which the society one lives and works in provides. But to belong, on top of that, to a community alien to that society, must be considered disgraceful.

Period, said Olausson.

But his lecture still didn't seem altogether perfected and finished. He began to glance at his watch, wasn't it time to leave for school soon? He got the disquieting feeling that he hadn't mastered his subject, hadn't prepared thoroughly, something that never used to happen to him.

I have nothing against the man Silberstein, he said helplessly, but surely he could be a little more approachable.

He imagined he heard part of the audience starting to titter disrespectfully. The irritation flared up inside him.

Not that I would in any way be dependent on his approachability, he tried, but because being approachable is a prerequisite for people who live under the same roof in the same society. He mustn't think that he can stay so damned independent!

He noticed that his listeners were astonished. He had obviously forgotten himself.

No no, he muttered, I can't be wrong, I quite simply can't be wrong.

I've been accused of prying, he said, I stand here defending myself against an ugly accusation of prying. They say that one should leave people alone. I am the first to endorse such a proposition. But an ostentatious silence, an ostentatious evasiveness, cannot be regarded as compatible with this principle. On the contrary, it must in fact be regarded as implying a hidden criticism of one's fellow human beings, as a very obvious way of stinging and wounding. Have I expressed myself clearly enough?

Silence.

Thank you, said Olausson. I see that I am finally beginning to be understood.

I will not allow the man's flagrant separateness to inflame my reactions, he continued.

What sorts of reaction?

A healthy, objective interest in people is certainly not a sensational reaction.

I am thus back at my starting point.

He sensed that it was time for summation and conclusion. It had been easy at the start, now it was complicated and difficult. He regretted that he had begun the lecture, but he had felt, after all, such a strong need for it. He hadn't suspected that the topic was so personal, that he would become so peculiarly agitated. He felt all at once that he loathed Silberstein even though he had started from such a detached and levelheaded interest. Silberstein had made himself ridiculous at *his* expense. But Silberstein was unfair. I'm certainly no dunce, he thought, but when you never get an answer in a discussion, it's easy to forget yourself.

Besides, the man is in fact altogether uninteresting; it's a waste of time to consider him.

I have attempted to elucidate the concepts in a subject that many may think is ephemeral and insignificant, he said. That, however, is perhaps not the case. In our relations with both the Jewish individual and the Jewish group, we are much too easily guided by emotions and non-objective viewpoints. If I have given any of you a somewhat clearer consciousness of this, I have surely done both you and Mr. Silberstein a service.

That devil won in the end, he thought. He got at my emotions. I'd better be on my guard. It's really an unpleasant business.

He is really and truly unpleasant.

With a feeling of relief, Schoolmaster Olausson saw that it was time to leave for school. He realized that it wouldn't be very nice for the children today. That was Mr. Silberstein's fault. One might say that life was unfair to make it Mr. Silberstein's fault, but that's how it was.

He was not a successful lecture topic.

And then too, he never looked like he washed properly.

It was time to go teach the dumb little brats the multiplication table.

6

He missed her.

The longing coiled inside him, wound around his heart and his bowels, tightened behind his forehead, made his eyelids ache; his eyes were wide open and he didn't want to blink, because on the inside of his eyelids was the image of her idiotic friendliness, which both tormented him and attracted him.

He laid his hand heavily on the telephone receiver. His hand was hairy and fleshy; where do I get all this flesh from, considering I hardly eat anything? Well, lift the receiver now, hand of mine! Speak, mouth! Cajole, tongue! Live life, Emanuel!

Or what if he were to give the clients a rest today? How about letting them think: Why doesn't Silberstein call? It's been a long while now and the jars are almost empty. Hollow sloshing in the bottles. So where is Silberstein! The industrious, the energetic businessman with the modern methods. The expert salesman. We'll have to give him a call.

His hand rested on the receiver. He smiled. Now it's going to ring, he thought. Now they'll start. Now. Soon they'll have to wait their turn.

Silence.

Silence.

This hour when there's a slight glistening in bottle and jar: the morning sun, beaming in off the display window across the street and through the flaws in the whitewash. They should see my stock now. Now it looks tempting, even if a bit dusty. The dust and the sun vanish at the same time. The dust.

This was the hour when he ought to do something about the dust.

His hand rested on the receiver.

Silence.

Then his own voice: Hallo!

Hallo in the silence.

First carefully. Then louder. Then a cry. Hallo in the silence! Then a roar. Hallo in the silence!

Sweat broke out on his forehead. His fingers on the receiver turned white. His upper body swayed. Under the table his boots squeaked against each other.

Hallo!!

Hallo!!!

Hallo, sir! Hallo, Sire! Hallo, Lord!

Lord, this is your humblest little pomade-Jew speaking, your most miserable little jar-Moses calling from his perfumed hole in the cellar.

I don't expect an answer. I don't ask the switchboard for messages about your silence. I play with your existence as I play with your absence. That you don't exist is a matter of complete indifference to me. That I exist is a matter of complete indifference to you. Thus we can without difficulty or complications maintain a sort of harmless phone relationship.

What do you do with my secret hilarity?

What are you doing about my unconcealed anxiety?

I ask you: Who was this Silberstein that you had to destroy him so completely?

For certainly it's a ruined man who's sitting here performing his worn-out variety numbers for you.

This favorite old number: that one has hands, organs, senses, affections, passions like everyone else. That one is fed with food, hurt with weapons, subject to diseases and healed by medicines. That one bleeds, laughs and dies just like the rest of humanity and that it nonetheless happens in an essentially different way. That the great similarity is a sign of the great injustice that makes everything different. This old number, Lord, that has never made the slightest impression on you.

You know that I have a very large repertoire.

We have the memory repertoire.

We have the future repertoire.

We have the question repertoire.

We have the prosecutor's repertoire.

We have the defense attorney's repertoire.

We have the judge's repertoire.

We really have tons in our jars and bottles.

Just think of all our fairy tales and legends. Should I tell you one? As long as I'm not interrupted by the telephone.

Once upon a time there was a little boy. He had big, dark eyes and beautiful curly hair and naturally he was the apple of his parents' eye. His nose had the finest curve of any in that whole little narrow street and no one could come up with such funny and clever games as he could or mimic the rabbi better or more comically. Since he was also unusually nice for a child, there was no reason why life shouldn't turn out well for him. Precocious at both Hebrew and mathematics, he inspired great hopes; and he lied and stole just enough and without going too far, so he had no moral flaws to speak of.

The little boy lived in a city where there were a great many pigeons, but it seemed the birds hadn't learned to find their way to the alley where he lived with his family: perhaps they realized they would scarcely find room there, since there was always an unbearable crush of people. You could see the pigeons gliding, up in the crack of sky that shone blue, high up between the buildings, but they never dropped down between the walls of the houses, and instead always sought out more open places for their promenades and gatherings. The boy had dared to go down to the square one time to get close to the birds, but other children, the outsiders, had yelled at him so coarsely and cruelly that he had hurried back to the alleyway.

For a long time after that he went around dreaming of pigeons, in much the same way that boys nowadays dream about puppies, I should think. He often stood in the alley with his face turned upwards, he didn't notice if people laughed at him or bumped into him, he stood there with an expectant expression in his eyes and around his gaping mouth, so that some of the wise elders thought they could see in him an unusual gift for piety.

Then one day a pigeon collided with the wall way up at the top of the building and fell down into the alleyway. The boy wasn't at all surprised; he picked up the pigeon in his hands as if he'd been expecting it to arrive for a long time, and carried it into his parents' house. He felt the bird's heart beating against his palms; aside from that the bird was completely still.

Heart, little heart, he whispered.

Surely you recognize the tale, Lord? It's the usual sentimental bit about the boy and the bird. In every country. From time immemorial.

The boy felt the bird's heart and his own and the bird's heart was beating much faster.

The boy felt his human heart beating, calmly and steadily. And in that moment he felt great piety, Lord.

And the boy dreamt of nursing the bird so that one day it would be able to fly again, but you know how it was, the bird's wing was broken. And the boy's father dashed the bird hard against a stone wall so it wouldn't suffer anymore, and the boy's father did right.

And the boy saw the bird's blood splatter across the wall, the blood that had flowed through the little ticking heart, the blood that one fateful day he would forget to take account of, and the blood filled him with infinite tenderness, and he wept.

You mustn't be sad, little Shylock, said his father – for that was the name of the boy who later became such a skillful usurer – you mustn't be sad, because there is no city in the world that has so many pigeons as Venice.

Do you understand that fairy tale, Lord?

We can take a second one too, we'll grab the chance now that the telephone is quiet anyway.

Once upon a time there was a Jewish shoemaker who gave his son the name Ahasuerus. His wife didn't want to go along with this at all, since such a terribly unfortunate fate was associated with the name, but the shoemaker got his way.* He thought that the name Ahasuerus would serve his son as a reminder and a warning: that's what happens to the Jew who is not good and merciful, that's how we wander forever through the world, that's how poor a foundation our house stands on, and our misdeeds visit greater punishment on us than misdeeds do on any other people, because you, Lord, have indeed chosen us.

Little Ahasuerus heard continually about his big namesake's dreadful fate.

And this, Lord, is the tale of little Ahasuerus's dread.

There was no child as nice as little Ahasuerus. No one could perform as many good deeds as he could. No one was as eager to lead blind people across the street, prop up the crippled, help up the fallen, bear others' burdens, steady the drunkards and take care of the careless. He became so meddlesome it was downright irritating.

At night he had nightmares.

He dreamt of lemminglike processions of the halt, the lame, the blind, the deaf, the misshapen and the deranged, and they were all screaming: Ahasuerus, don't fail me! Beware, Ahasuerus, if you reject me! Ahasuerus! Ahasuerus!

Little Ahasuerus was bathed in sweat as he ran alongside the grotesque procession. Little Ahasuerus was bathed in sweat as he lay in his bed dreaming.

He dreamt.

He dreamt that he was lying on the ground looking up into the sky and that he knew a moment's peace. Then he heard shuffling steps. He clamped his eyes shut desperately. I'm sleeping, he

---

*Ahasuerus: the name of the Wandering Jew in the medieval legend.
— R. G.

screamed, can't you see that I'm sleeping! But the shuffling of steps sounded closer and closer. Little Ahasuerus stuck his fingers in his ears. I don't hear anything, he screamed, I'm sleeping! And suddenly the world was completely quiet. For a long while Ahasuerus lay still, then he cautiously opened his eyes. The sun was shining on him, everything was very warm, everything was very quiet. Then all at once a terrible laugh rang out, it roared and swept over him, little Ahasuerus writhed under it – it has nothing to do with me, he screamed – but he had to look, he was a prisoner of his name. Far away he saw a gigantic man standing with an enormous cross high above his head. That's who was laughing. But the laugh was transformed into a frightful grimace and suddenly the giant threw the great cross at little Ahasuerus. It came flying toward him, infinitely slow and somehow full of evil intentions. Little Ahasuerus lay there as if paralyzed, he wanted to get up and run away – and he would probably manage to escape, the cross was flying so slowly – but he just lay there waiting, and now, now the cross was going to crush him, and the scream stayed locked in his throat and he thought I have to wake up so the scream can get out and now I'm waking up and now I'm screaming and he woke up and screamed.

Tired and trembling, little Ahasuerus got out of bed and went into the streets to search for his merciful deeds. He staggered, his legs wouldn't carry him properly. The city was full of neglect and menace and Ahasuerus was filled with dread. The heat lay heavily between the buildings and the world shimmered.

The streets were strangely deserted and little Ahasuerus went along as if sleepwalking. But in the distance he heard a strange rushing sound and knew that somewhere in that direction the good deed must be waiting for him. He walked toward the rushing sound and the heat ached behind his forehead. Far off down the street he saw an old Jew come running with his sidelocks flapping comically about his ears and his palms turned to the heavens. They're burning it, screamed the old man, those devils are burning our synagogue, and Ahasuerus walked on as if he had heard nothing.

Then all at once, right in his path, an obese woman with dull eyes and wild hair, staggering under the burden of her fat, her eyes pale blue – like dirty water, thought Ahasuerus. She spread her enormous arms toward him, her legs far apart like a pair of enormous pillars. Help me, little man, she wailed, I can't make it over there, I want to join in, have mercy on me!

As if she had recited a spell, little Ahasuerus stopped and took his place right up against the gigantic woman. The stench of sweat and onions overwhelmed him and he felt like vomiting when she lay her arm heavily across his shoulders. Oh, how kind you are, she said, you're so kind to help me watch them burning down the temple of those idol-worshipping swine.

The stench, the heat, the unbearable weight – Ahasuerus prayed to God for strength, and His mercy made his legs strong. The peculiar pair tottered through the streets. Give me that fagot there, little friend, she asked, I want to help them. Ahasuerus leaned the shapeless woman against the wall of a building and picked up the fagot from the gutter. He led her forward gently and carefully, in one hand carrying fuel for the conflagration.

The tremendous fire, the tremendous crowd that was screaming and surging, the enormous blaze inside his eyelids. He cleared a path for her through the throng of people. It's too hot, she screamed, and the sweat washed over her quivering face, I can't go on – you throw it, little man, have mercy on me! Little Ahasuerus let go of the woman, she toppled toward him and down onto the street. Run, she cried, go burn it! Little Ahasuerus ran forward to the blaze, he heard people screaming, he threw his fagot. Then he turned around, he saw everyone staring at him, but the fat woman was lying there keeping her eyes closed as if she were sleeping.

Then little Ahasuerus walked through the crowd where many were weeping and many were laughing, he walked through the empty streets, he walked and walked, he walked out of the city and since then no one has seen him, have you, Lord?

Silberstein shut his eyes, folded his arms on the table and laid his heavy head on them, the dust danced above him, and everything was gray. He listened to his breathing, he drooled on his jacket sleeve, tired, indifferent. Telling fairy tales was a poor way to kill time, poor tales for a poor listener, and tiring besides.

His heart beat a little too hard, it pounded in its cavity, that cavity that still felt a pang or two, perhaps for her, the importuning, the ridiculously meddlesome woman, with her library and her avid friendliness. He saw her before him now – he mustn't shut his eyes anymore, the longing mustn't get a hold on him.

He got up, with his finger he drew a line in the dust on the table, then he went around the store and began moving jars from shelf to shelf; it was a completely meaningless task. System, he muttered, got to have another system here, another, system, system with a different method, a different sort of system than before, of another kind, not better, not worse, a different one, just different.

Here he truly had his hands full. Here there was really no problem getting the day to pass. Here there were plenty of jars that could be shifted around, and so many bottles! And crates that weren't empty, and crates that were empty. If it got too lonely and sad, moreover, he could start rattling everything, he could fill the whole store with clatter, with activity that would be heard even out on the street, a lively business, this one, no doubt about it.

Silberstein held a jar in front of his mouth and laughed. The shiny lid gave back a blurred reflection, he laughed into the label instead, one Silberstein was more than enough.

Oh, I understand so perfectly, Mr. Silberstein . . .

He heard her voice as clearly as if she'd been there and spoken to him. Dammit! Dammit! Can't I keep her away from me?

Do I have to tell more stories?

Let us tell the tale of trusting Sara.

Silberstein sat down again. He sat thumping the tabletop with his hand for a while. He thumped a comfortable little pain into his fist. Then he let his hand rest.

Let us tell the tale of trusting Sara.

Lord, do you remember Sara?

Who thought she'd received such a beautiful promise from you – do you remember her?

Who sat forever weeping over the infinite void, and suddenly thought she heard your voice, just when the most intense panic had gripped her heart.

What was it she thought you said?

Sara, in my infinitude rests the world, rest thou in my infinite world; the arms of my infinity embrace you, my hand is touching your aching brow, and my hand is a promise.

And your words gave Sara great calm.

And she thought that everyone rested in your infinite embrace, and she included all those resting ones in her great trust.

And she smiled always.

And filled with her infinite trust she went out among the others who were as young as she was and whom she called her friends, and she felt as if it was you who were sending her out among them so that she might be happy.

And she was very pretty, and her breasts had just become like doves, as I believe it says in your song of songs.

And the boys never called her anything but the Jewess, and she smiled.

And the girls called her Miss Hooknose, and she smiled.

And the boys said that they wanted to see if she had more hair between her legs than the others, because that's what people said about Jewesses.

And she refused to show them, and she smiled.

Then they yelled dirtier and dirtier words at her.

And they tied her to a tree, and they told her they were doing this for Jesus' sake, and she smiled even though it was such a strange game.

And they shot at her with their bows, and this was even in a time between persecutions.

And one of their blunt arrows shot into her eye, and she screamed.

And they all ran away and she stood there alone for a long time, tied to the tree, and screamed.

Later her brother Emanuel often sat by her bed and stared into the white bandage over her eye and held her hand and heard her say that they hadn't meant it to come to this.

For you had filled her with trust.

And her blood was poisoned and the fever took hold and she died, resting in the infinite embrace of your kindness.

And her life was a tale that was told but not heard, and everyone was filled with pity for the ones who had to suffer remorse because they had done wrong.

Lord, do you remember Sara?

Silberstein, Silberstein, you and all your stories!

He closed his eyes and considered Sara, unalterably beautiful as only the dead can be, he looked at her without sorrow and without longing, for thus does life wear out all our feelings. Thank you Sara, he muttered, Miss Svensson doesn't disturb me anymore. You are helpful. But he felt that he shouldn't have mentioned that woman's name, now she was there again, insisting.

Oh good God, he whispered forlornly, do you really want more stories, won't you have enough soon?

He searched for a story that would be able to keep her off, but he was tired and muddled; this is a curious version of the Thousand and One Nights, he thought.

The tale of Aaron, then?

Aaron was the name of a rich merchant. When he felt that a time of persecution was approaching, he gave away all his property and set out on the road. And he did not grieve for all that he had lost.

Then he came one day to a woman and the urge took him and she was a good woman and he stayed there. And he told her who he was and she was very fond of him.

The persecution came and the people in the area began to

whisper about the man whom the woman had at her place. But the woman loved him intensely. And Aaron loved the woman and stayed there with her.

But this persecution was a protracted one.

And in the woman's eyes Aaron thought he saw fear awakening, but he wasn't sure.

And the people in the area were no longer whispering, they were shouting.

Then Aaron said to the woman that it was time for him to leave, but shame forced her to ask him to stay.

And the people in the area were no longer shouting, they were screaming.

Then the woman's love couldn't hold up anymore, she no longer loved him, but she wouldn't admit this, even to herself.

And she stood firm for the sake of her dignity.

And fear seized Aaron so that he didn't dare to leave.

And they no longer went out in the daytime.

At night when she thought he was sleeping she looked at him and whispered, I hate you, and the words passed her lips without her meaning them to, and she wouldn't believe them because of her dignity. And Aaron heard the words but pretended he was sleeping and wouldn't believe them because of his fear.

And in the morning when they awoke, many of the windowpanes were smashed, and they stuffed rags in the holes so that the room grew dark.

And now their hatred for each other made them inseparable.

And Aaron said that he must go and the woman that he must stay and neither of them meant a word of it.

And each night the people crept closer to the house.

And the people banged on the doors and threw stones into the rooms, and inside, both of them aged quickly. And both of them had become ugly and nasty.

And the woman felt that she hated all strangers, and as for her dignity, she had forgotten it.

And one night when the people were clamoring outside, she got up from her bed, took the longest knife from the kitchen drawer and stabbed it into Aaron's breast. And this was the death of Aaron, who had once been a rich merchant.

And with the bloody knife in her hand she stepped onto the front stairs and cried out to the people that she had just killed the Jewish swine.

In silence the people regarded the woman with the tangled gray hair as she stood there in her long nightdress with the knife raised above her head.

And when the rejoicing finally broke out, the woman felt a great relief.

Afterwards many songs were written about her and she became a symbol and a saint, and her house was held in veneration.

That is the tale of the rich merchant, Aaron.

Silberstein sat there for a moment. The smile on his face was even more crooked than usual. He looked into himself. Then he sighed a sigh of release and took hold of the telephone receiver.

He no longer missed her.

7

The workday, as it was called, finally came to an end. Shut the door, turn the key, the few steps up to the street.

And the whole day he had succeeded in keeping people away from him, even the clients. It had been a successful day in every respect.

Silberstein felt almost exhilarated as he stood on the street and caught his breath for a moment. It might even be pleasant to walk the short stretch between the store and the block called The

Mirage. And what if he were to lengthen the route! What if he were to make a detour for once!

He stood there rocking back and forth, his body was moving but his feet were still motionless on the pavement, as if they were waiting for a decision. He put his hand on the slouch hat and turned his face upwards. Indeed, the weather wasn't bad. A feeling of freedom rose up inside him, he couldn't understand where it came from or why.

Miss Svensson, he said and laughed, and didn't feel the slightest sting of anxiety. He felt as if he'd suddenly mastered existence and the art of living, all that stuff you found stupid advice about in stupid newspapers and silly handbooks.

He started walking, and he noticed that his steps dragged less than usual. That's thanks to all my fine stories, he thought, I'm not bad at storytelling if I say so myself. Two-three good stories a day and I'll be able to talk to people and mix with people with the proper detachment.

He made his way down to the more heavily trafficked streets, he was looking for crowds. He bumped against people coming the other way, was actually rubbing up against his dear fellow humans and all the while muttering and singing, now he wasn't afraid to attract attention, not at all.

He strode forward, straightened his back, looked straight ahead and all around and didn't stare at the pavement. This won't last long, he thought, but the thought was clear and outside him, it had no effect on him.

Mr. Silberstein out strolling, he thought, what's so remarkable about that? How do you pass the evening after a well-spent day of work? You go have a bite to eat, isn't that right, Silberstein? You're hungry, you have no food at home, well then, you go to a restaurant.

He stopped in the middle of the sidewalk, clapped his hands together and rubbed the palms against each other in a gesture of appetite. Then he set his course.

At the entrance to the restaurant he wasn't so sure. What am I trying to force on myself, he thought, and why am I doing it? He slumped. But he couldn't just stand there staring, after all, either one thing or the other, don't stand there like a hesitant beggar at a kitchen door.

He stepped in, his gaze on the floor. Cloakroom attendant, head waiter, waiter, tablecloth, menu, he stammered out his order, then stared at the buttons on his vest, gave it a tug so it wouldn't wrinkle up so much over his belly – didn't do any good.

What was taking so long? Why didn't they bring him anything? He was probably the butt of an insult. He didn't dare to look up, the staff were surely smirking at him. And the other guests were surely in on the joke. He listened intently. He didn't hear a sound. Was it deathly quiet throughout the large hall? Not a voice speaking. Not the clink of a fork and knife against a plate. Had they even stopped eating? Were they sitting there open-mouthed, in the midst of chewing, just staring at him? He was sweating, he felt how disgusting it was. Get up and leave, that was the only thing to do, but the walk to the door was endless. He saw his dark, hairy hands lying folded on the white tablecloth. He felt that he was unbearably heavy. Imagine if the chair should give way and crash to pieces under him. In that case the thing to do was just to lie still and pretend he had fainted, the way an animal plays dead, and let them carry him out, what a relief, if only it would happen, if only the roof would cave in and the walls collapse so everything could be over and he could escape. He wondered if one of the large chandeliers was hanging right above his head, already he could feel the horrible pain in his bald crown, but didn't dare to look up now in the terrible silence just before – and then all at once the music began to play, the silence was broken, the food was served, beer and schnapps arrived at the table, and it had all passed.

He sat there awhile, relaxing, breathing deeply, his gaze on his vest. He wasn't hungry, the smell of the piece of meat sickened him. He glanced up at the glass of schnapps, then reached out his hand and took hold of it, his hand trembled a little as he brought the glass to his mouth. He swallowed it all in one gulp, managed to suppress the cough, grimaced, shut his eyes, passed his left hand over his face, then sat still again.

He waited.

His throat burned and his stomach ached a little, it wasn't pleasant yet. He gave himself a shake, then went to work on the meat, was suddenly eating very fast, drinking beer. Another one, he muttered when the waiter took away the empty schnapps glass. Another one, he said when he got no answer. Another schnapps, I said, he repeated when the waiter said Beg-pardon? That was a hell of a lot of chat to get a schnapps, he thought, and now he was finally beginning to feel comfortable.

Now it was good to eat. Now it was comfortable being here. He looked up at the waiter, lifted the glass off the tray, raised the schnapps to his mouth, and then down with it at once, no shilly-shallying here. It didn't burn this time, it tasted good, everything was good, the food, the liquor, the music, this was a splendid restaurant; he looked around.

He was looking around.

I'm looking around. It's not beautiful here, but it's congenial, isn't it, Silberstein? The people look like they're enjoying themselves, they look friendly and contented, don't they, Silberstein? And up here in the section nearest the entrance, artists, musicians, actors, the types you see in the tabloids. You're sitting among celebrities, Silberstein.

Coffee and cognac, and then a brandy and soda, please. Yes I can order that later, yes, that's right, waiter.

You've lost the assured restaurant manner you had in the old days, Emanuel Silberstein, and therefore you're pretending to be a little simpler than you are so as not to seem snooty. You're also going to leave a somewhat larger tip than necessary, and the waiter is going to despise you for it. That's how life is, and you can say that about everything, even about Emanuel Silberstein's character, fate, and development. That's how life is.

And here they sit, and they eat, and they drink, and they talk, and then they drink some more, and then they go out to the little room opposite the cloakroom and there they stand in long rows and piss, and later they go home and they've had a merry evening, the whole thing is revolting. No it isn't, Silberstein, it's cozy and friendly here, it's good to be here. The women are beautiful and the men dignified, the hell they are, people are ugly, and you yourself are the ugliest one, Emanuel, amazing you aren't shown the door, you must be ruining people's appetite and reducing sales, look around, the owner must be standing in one corner or another, can't you feel his greedy, critical eyes on you?

I'll have the brandy and soda, so the owner's eyes will be friendly. I didn't say anything, waiter, I just asked if I could have the brandy and soda now, this is the thirsty hour, marvelous thirst's marvelous hour, time for the great limbering up.

The hour when you fall apart and become approachable.

Again relief. His fingers around the cold glass. Rattle the ice. Slosh the liquor around. Look thoughtful. Look pleased. Look musical when you listen to the music. Give a small laugh as if you happened to think of something funny.

He gave a laugh.

Good God, he'd forgotten to cover his mouth with his hand, everyone must have seen those disgusting little brown stumps, was he beginning to lose control?

The hour when you fall apart and become approachable.

Hi there, old Jew.

He started. Someone had spoken to him. He looked up into a grinning face that he thought he recognized though he knew he'd never met the young man who stood swaying beside his table.

Hi there, old Jew. My name is Asp. I'm an actor, goddammit, that's why you recognize me. Can I sit down here? I love old Jews.

I'm a famous Judeophile, I can't see a Jew without leaping over and conversing.

He sat down and Silberstein looked into a fair, somewhat pasty face that must still have been quite handsome a couple of years ago. The man was young, blond and under the influence, and the liquor had removed all definition from his regular features.

And now, old Jew, let's have a whiskey together, said Asp, and he signalled and ordered. A Jew with a whiskey, he continued, what a sight! You Jews are lousy boozers, that's the only thing I have against you. Otherwise I'll be damned if you aren't better than everybody else, which isn't saying much of course but it's something. Well say something now, goddammit!

Silberstein, said Silberstein.

He felt a strange desire to please, he felt ingratiating. I'm falling, he thought, it's the liquor's fault, I shouldn't drink.

Well hell, said Asp, is it the old codger Silversteen one has the honor of meeting up with, what an honor! Then he changed his tune and grew sentimental. Yes, don't think for a minute that I'm not being serious, he said, for a drunken second-class actor it's an honor to down a whiskey with the representative of an ancient culture. Skoal to you, Silversteen!

Silberstein raised his glass and smiled, they clinked glasses, they drank. He was sure that Asp was not putting him on, at least he thought he was sure of it. It's the liquor's fault, he thought again, it takes away my protective uncertainty, it's dangerous, I've got to watch out. But the thought was somehow far away from him, it didn't touch him, it was just there, like writing on the wall.

Skoal to you, Asp, said Silberstein.

He had immediately raised his glass again. He sat smiling openly at the actor. He was socializing.

This is one hell of an old Jew – a champ at swallowing, laughed Asp. In your honor, Silversteen!

Silberstein suddenly plunged into the honor, dove down into

the word honor, and he felt he was drowning in it. It closed like a wave over his bald crown.

Honor, he said, you whelp, you see before you a man who is miles and years distant from honor and who doesn't miss it. The very word makes me gag and cough.

I'm talking, he thought.

I cough, he continued, I hawk and I spit. What does honor have to give me and what do I have to give to honor. Equally little, we're even.

My dear Asp, you and your actor's honor! You who collect praise and mess around pasting it in scrapbooks, you can go glut on your headline-honor! You can go wallow in your Pass-with-Honors and swill up your newspaper-honor!

I'm talking, he thought.

Asp, dear boy, he went on, for me honor is a danger and danger is an honor and therefore I throw honor on the garbage pile and wrap myself in my lack of honor like a field mouse in his grayness. Freed from honor I slink into my hole to sleep, eat, and die. I make it a point of honor to free myself from honor. The only thing I demand on that score is to be made an honorary mouse. You can be an honorary Jew, Asp, a Judeophilic Honorary Jew with neat sufferings honorably engraved on your chest, decorated, wreathed, admired.

I'm talking, he thought.

Don't feel sorry for yourself, Jew-codger, said Asp.

In your honor, Asp, and skoal to you, laughed Silberstein, it's an honor for me to be able to share a table with an actor, no matter what kind you are, I am a friend of actors, you see, a Thespiophile, that's gallant of me, isn't it, really something to boast about, for actors are after all so despised and the theater is an ancient cultural institution – here's to you, in honor of you, maker of culture!

I'm talking, he thought.

They always say Jews are clever, said Asp.

No offense meant, my dear Asp, said Silberstein, I'll treat you to a whiskey, I'm going to cherish your company, a friend of Jews with a friend of actors, such a thing mustn't be allowed to slip away these days, converse with me, Asp, be entertaining, don't fritter away this sociable hour.

He noticed that he was tipsy, Asp's face reeled, and before it reeled his own grotesquely magnified and distorted face, disintegrated into its wretched component parts.

Converse with me, Asp, he repeated.

Sure I'll converse with you, old Jew, said Asp, as long as you're pleasant and grateful and don't put too much strain on my self-esteem. Sure I'll converse with you. It's just that you're so damned ugly that it's going to take a hell of a lot of drink. Yes, I can say something like that without being horrible, because I have my own special charm, don't I, old man?

The table came toward him and dove away, Silberstein understood that he had nodded. The boy did indeed have a careless charm; that he would certainly not deny. He heard himself talking, he heard Asp talking, but he didn't really know about what anymore, he wasn't listening to either of them. Deep inside himself he was totally lucid and very sad, he could feel it: very weak, very much alone, very miserable. What is this Fall going to end up costing me, he thought; if the poison of socializing gets into my blood, what won't it cost me in the end.

I've got one hell of a talent, he heard Asp say, but I booze too much. I'm an alcoholic and I know it. They say that insight into your illness is supposed to help, but the hell it does! Nothing can help me. I guess you know all about that, old codger. It doesn't help you a goddamned bit that you know you're a Jew. You're a Jew just the same. Don't say anything, it won't do any good because I don't give a damn about logic. Logic exists for petits bourgeois and teetotalers. They think you can figure life out. We know you can't do that, you and me, Silversteen, because that's something that Jews and alcoholics know. That's why I like Jews even though they're lousy boozers. Skoal to you, Silversteen! I like you because you're a living violation of logic. Don't look so puzzled, I know very well what I'm saying, and I'm saying it damned well, because I have one hell of a talent, everyone says so and no one objects when I say so myself. I invent stories that are as fine as snuff and extraordinarily striking. Write it down, Asp, everyone says, but I don't write it down, I'm fooling them, and all my fine stories are gonna go to the grave together with yours truly. I'll tell you stories and you'll admire me, because Jews have a goddamned astounding gift for socializing. They can look admiring even when their hearts are aloof and contemptuous, which they are most of the time. I can't understand how you escaped the gas chambers! Imagine that I can fling out something like that without getting you mad – because I have my own special charm.

I'm not mad, said Silberstein. Keep conversing with me. It tickles my self-contempt not to answer you, it's first-rate.

I am a scoundrel, said Asp. I am a scoundrel with a sensitive conscience. It's only scoundrels, by the way, who have a sensitive conscience, because they're always pricking it with their villainy till it's tender. You have no idea what I can get up to. And what self-reproach I'm capable of. I'm really one hell of a guy, a truly fine person. I'm not the only one who says so, my friends say so too. I have a lot of friends. Everyone's got a Jesus complex and is going to save me – from liquor, from myself. When I've been too obnoxious I cry, that always gets them, because so few people dare to cry in front of someone else that they think it must mean a hell of a lot when you do it. They behold the depths. And it's true I'm damned unhappy. I can come up and cry at your place one day if you want. One day when I need to borrow money. Then you can have a chance to feel like Jesus, old Jew. That'd be fine, huh? Aren't I talking well? You have no idea how much I've got in me! Should we add it up? No we don't give a damn about that! Must be at least a liter. What an awakening tomorrow! Why should only certain people have to suffer? Why weren't you gassed? What sort of justice is that? Those others surely didn't look much viler than you? Let me know if you don't think this patter is amusing! I don't want to make you sad, I'm a Judeophile. Should I shed a few tears now and be lovable? I'm an alcoholic, I do all sorts of tricks for one more whiskey. I can even go to bed with you, but Jews are seldom queers. Besides, I'm a type that women go for, there are loads of females who want to save me. Besides, I don't know why I'm saying besides. I can arrange a female for you too if you want. Since you weren't gassed after all, you certainly ought to make sure to enjoy life a little, as long as it lasts. Life can have its own special charm, I tell you. Life and Asp have their own special charm. You understand, I hope, that I only say that bit about the gas because I like you so damned much. Anti-Semites never say things like that. They say personally I have nothing against Jews and then come seven pages of bad quasi science. Aren't I right? Just whisper a word about gas chambers to an anti-Semite and he'll get furiously upset and indignant. An anti-Semite is always profoundly moral. And I am profoundly immoral but in a pro-foundly moral way. By behaving immorally I keep my moral awareness alive. It may seem a bit strained but it's effective. If you know any anti-Semites I'll punch them in the mouth for you. I'm strong as hell, I still haven't boozed away my muscles. Here – feel.

Asp jumped up, danced around the table like a boxer in the ring, over to Silberstein, and stuck out his arm. Silberstein squeezed it. Hell of a muscle, he said, and now go sit down again. Are you bullying me, you Jew bastard, Asp screamed and knocked a glass off the table. A waiter came over. Sit down, he said to Asp, and Asp sat down obediently. I'm stronger than that oaf, he said, but I detest barroom brawls. A whiskey here, he yelled, but no one seemed to hear him. They think I've had too much, he said weari-ly, and I think I'll be damned if they aren't right. Besides, I have enough talent so I can talk without fuel.

Silberstein sat listening to the endless stream of words. The mixture of aggression and friendliness gave him a feeling of secu-rity, this Asp doesn't hide anything, he thought, all I need to do is listen to what he says, I don't have to give a damn about his tone of voice. It's nice. What's more he doesn't give a good goddamn about me, he only cares about playing the fool. He's the sort of contact I ought to have these days.

The sort of contact I ought to have! Have I managed to lose my footing so badly in one evening that I think I ought to have contacts? You're in danger, Silberstein. Maybe your splendid solitude is too much for you after all? Are you really sitting here grinning at this repulsive fellow opposite you and letting him flaunt his gas-chamber cynicism! Can't you ever get low enough to escape being afraid?

I'm going now, he said and was suddenly afraid of his intoxication.

Going home already, alcoholic-Jew, said Asp, order another whiskey, they'll give you one for sure, you're still steady on your feet and I'll drink it up for you. Don't shake your head like that, you'll lose your balance and you've got to have balance for two when we leave here – waiter I want to pay up! The devil heard *that*, nothing wrong with his hearing now, oh no. Here you go, ganymede. I have a colleague who's been to the university and he always says ganymede. Take a generous tip, goddammit, you can figure it out yourself. I probably would have cut a fine figure at a university too, gone there for years and years and learned to say ganymede with the right sort of drawl.

Asp unloaded bills from his pocket and laid them in a pile on the table.

I'm really stingy as a Jew, he said, and tomorrow when I wake up I'll shed a few tears over how much I've run through unnecessarily, and then I'll go around and cry up a little money from my friends and then I'll come here and drink away my regrets and lay the basis for new ones. Can't you treat me, old Jew, so I can get through tomorrow dry-eyed? Now I scared you something terrible, huh? Now your little Jew-heart gave a squeeze, huh? Now you clenched your fist around your purse and thought we've got to watch out for Asp the actor. Waiter, I'll pay the whole thing! Serves you right, old Jew, now you can sit there and be ashamed of your stinginess. Yes, I'll pay for everything, my treat, I want to! I want to make you happy, and you're damned sure to be happy if you get out of here scot-free, you Jew bastard.

Why is it so nice to be called a Jew bastard, thought Silberstein, why is it so nice? But he couldn't even manage to try for an answer. When they got up he could feel that he was drunk. Asp walked quickly ahead of him, as straight and steady as if he hadn't had a drop. Silberstein was very drunk and very tired. Is it a long way home, he thought, it mustn't be a long way home. I don't want to walk alone and drunk through the streets.

The cool night air. How long have I been sitting in there, he thought, it must be a very long time. Well, are you coming, old codger, he heard Asp call, and he saw him standing and grinning a short way up the street. He staggered over toward him. I'll prop you up, said Asp, a drunken old Jew, this is a successful night for a Judeophile.

He took Silberstein under the arm. A pang of dread shot through Silberstein at the sudden touch. I've let him in, he thought, he's gotten too close to me.

And all the way through the streets a feeling of danger, and Asp's voice that kept grinding away next to him and that he knew he would soon miss, and the missing that would continue in the morning and frighten him all the next day and for several days after that, and everything was very confused, and he didn't know anymore what he wanted.

I'm drunk, he thought, it's just that I'm drunk, but he knew it wasn't true; he felt perfectly lucid, it was just his body that didn't want to behave.

I'll be damned if I don't like you, yelled Asp and the words filled Silberstein with panic, you're the only one in this shit-hole of a city that a body can socialize with, you're the only one who's learned that life is a lottery in which one person becomes a Jew and another an alcoholic and that it's nothing but a goddamned lottery, the whole deal. If you're nice I'll take you upstairs and tuck you in bed and lecture on the Aspean lottery theory, and you'll see that it's a fine theory and how damned unfair everything is and I'm a lot more talented than most of the big winners.

Here's where I live, said Silberstein, and he didn't dare to look into Asp's eyes.

That's fine, said Asp, I'll come up for a nightcap.

I don't have anything in the house, Silberstein said and fumbled with the keys.

What the hell are you talking about, screamed Asp, haven't you got anything in the house? He began to cry. Let me come up with you anyway, I'm so lonely. No, said Silberstein, not tonight. And Asp screamed Jew bastard and Jewish swine, and Silberstein got the entrance door open and got it shut again. And when he was finally inside his apartment he was breathing very heavily. And he walked over to the window and looked down into the street and he saw Asp standing there crying under a streetlight. And Silberstein felt the emptiness of his rooms and the emptiness reeled, so he had to lie down on the bed with his clothes on.

He sits in the restaurant every single evening, he thought, and I'm going to go back there to meet him and he's a creep and he's detestable.

I'm going to go back there, was the last thing he thought before he fell asleep.

After that there were many mornings when he woke up with his clothes on, it seemed to him.

It seemed to him there were many evenings when he went down to the restaurant to let himself be insulted by Asp and to pay his checks, just small loans that I have no intention of paying back, as Asp said.

It seemed to him there were many evenings when Asp walked him to the entrance door and cried because there was no more liquor and because he wasn't allowed to come upstairs. And the room reeled when he lay down on top of the bed but had stopped when he woke up early in the morning with aching eyeballs and a foul taste in his mouth and Asp's taunts ringing, whispering and blaring someplace in the back of his head. He lay there awhile and repeated them with his dry lips: old Jew, Jewish swine, Jew-cadaver, Jew bastard, Jew-turd, all these invectives that gave him a strange relief: no property, no dignity, no danger.

They can't take anything away from me, Asp is cutting away the last remnants that I thought I'd want to protect.

He lay there with aching temples, he was too old to drink so much liquor. But the ache had no ominous meaning, on the contrary, it was fine, it took away all other meanings, it was something to keep occupied with until it was time for him to drag himself to the store.

Age claims its due, he thought, and it was a pleasant thought, because to grow old was to burn down and still keep living, it was to have awareness without anxiety and without pain, to be a part of things and yet not a part.

He lay there awhile and thought of Asp, poor detestable Asp, who still had all his vanity. He considered Asp's pasty face, it approached, it receded, at every distance it was equally vague,

equally vacant, just a bundle of expressions, most of them pretentious. The look of the misunderstood genius, the look of the misunderstood actor, the look of the brilliant conversationalist, the
look of the brilliant actor, a series of expressions that replaced one
another quickly and without transition, and that somehow never
originated in any face, only in the parts of a face, eyebrows, the
corners of a mouth, all the pieces that anyone can wave around
however he likes if only he takes the trouble to learn.

He lay there listening to Asp's voice, it too was vague, somewhat shrill and whining, with a scratchy edge to it and a light
nasal twang, a voice it would be hard to mimic because it so lacked
distinctiveness.

It seemed to him there were many mornings when he lay listening to Asp's voice this way and considering his face, and these
mornings were more real than the evenings when he sat opposite
him and saw and heard him. It seemed to him there were many,
but were there really so many? Everything from those times was as
vague as Asp, as elusive, almost treacherous.

Is that restaurant really there, he would think, does it really
exist, does Asp, do our strange conversations? What about the
hangover, then? Perhaps just the aftereffects of a nightmare. The
taste of liquor in my mouth? Is it the taste of liquor? Maybe just
hunger and dried-out old man.

Why not just erase Asp from my life, like everything else?

He lay there playing with his thoughts, but the thoughts
weren't real either. They had no significance.

Is Asp helping to distance me from reality, is that why I find
him so agreeable?

He lay there trying to recall Asp's monologues. They were as far
away as everything else. It was only the invectives he could hear
whenever he wanted to, without any effort at all, they rang inside
him as a reminder of a reality and that reality's absolute indifference.

I'm getting philosophical, he thought, it's the liquor, liquor
makes a person into a philosopher, into the most comfortable

thing of all: a bad philosopher. If there's anything I've striven to be all my life, it's a bad philosopher. What ambitions!

Nobody feels as good as a bad philosopher.

Therefore I'm feeling good . . .

And am just as sloppy in my logic, it's marvelous, my inner life is getting more and more comfortable. That Asp is not at all bad company.

I am a philosopher, I haven't landed in bad company, so no one can have any complaints against me. I grow finer by the minute. I'm developing.

He had to laugh – very carefully, on account of his fragile head. He pressed his fingers against his eyes and laughed softly, contentedly. Then he lay there awhile waiting for some sort of backlash, but it didn't come, all that happened was that he got sleepy.

Sleepy.

He yawned, lay there awhile and waited for sleep to return, but it didn't come, and in fact he'd known all along that it wouldn't. The slight irritation at the ends of his nerves, in his skin, kept him awake. It would keep him awake all day, even when his head fell heavily against the tabletop in the store and his breathing grew slow and wheezing.

It seemed to him there were many mornings when he finally got up and ran his large palms over his suit, which got more and more wrinkled each day and which he would decide each day to change, only to break the resolution with a sigh because it was so gratifyingly unimportant.

The liquor is making me apathetic, he thought, that's just fine, tiredness, I want to be tired. Asp is tiresome, there's no better company for me.

But his cheerfulness was gone. A little while ago he had lain there laughing, where was the laughter now? Oh well, no one can laugh all day, not even the silliest giggler. One mustn't ask for too much, that was the goal of all self-discipline, and the goal of his self-instruction was not to ask for anything at all.

It seemed to him there were many mornings when the laughter abandoned him this way and he had to reason with himself so as not to miss it. What exercises, he thought; isn't a person ever fully trained? Even in the simplest, the most elementary things? Truly, this is a long and difficult road to travel. Truly, man's path is paved with vanities on which he stumbles whether his gaze is on the heavens or on the ground. Truly, it is difficult to keep the essential nothingness continually before one's eyes.

It seemed to him there were many mornings when he talked to himself like a preacher, with many truly's and pious nods, a deceptive method through which his amusement led him to indispensable insights. Everything repeated itself, like the figures in a dance; the bear is jogging around in his cage, he thought, I'm like an old ballad with countless verses, and every morning we start the ballad over from the beginning, I would certainly be one hell of a case if I hadn't soon learned it by heart so it flowed out of me without all the little nervous hesitations.

All the little pricks and stings, when his memory threatened to dive down into another existence, a vanished and different one that he must not miss, because longing can really make an old caged bear do foolish things, even if it's only to attract attention by rattling the bars.

All the little nervous hesitations.

It seemed to him there were many mornings . . .

In the daytime at work . . .

He had begun to work better, more effectively, he needed more money, of course. He needed – it was frightening, but he shoved the thought aside, it'll be over soon, it's just temporary. He made phone calls more eagerly, he cajoled, he embellished his pitch, he was almost aggressive. There was a higher turnover of jars and bottles, his foul pomades were rubbed into more of the city's scalps. Now and then, as if in a game, he would walk around sniffing out his fragrances on the city streets, those sweet smells that now gave him not only the bare necessities of life but also its luxury, its festivity. The thought was so extraordinarily comical that he had to chuckle at it: is old Silberstein starting to find his work entertaining, he thought, and chuckled some more.

Asp dropped in on him at the store occasionally, to borrow money or talk nonsense. He sat there nonchalantly perched on a crate, with a dry mouth and superficial despair in his eyes, now and then gave a quick guffaw. His fair hair was long and hung down in his eyes, he tossed it back with his head.

A couple of tens, he would say, I'm in a damned bad way. I'm taking advantage of you, but you like that, you really eat it up. If I get three tens I'll treat you to a whiskey tonight, so don't say I'm not generous, you old cheapskate. What's more I have ideas on running the business here that I can sell you for next to nothing. That made you nervous, huh? What if there are millions buried in the skull of an actor! But you probably don't want to have millions, you're too fucking refined for that. Poor and snobbish is your number. A little jar-Jew on a back street, that's just perfect, it has all the opium charm of myth. I'm not in particularly good form today, I know, but you can't have everything for a couple of tens, and if you want to be entertained by a professional you'll have to pay accordingly, you should have understood that by now, you fount of wisdom.

Don't get offended now, you know I'm fond of you.

It doesn't matter, said Silberstein.

What doesn't matter, asked Asp, what I'm saying or that I'm fond of you? I'm going to be pissed off whichever one you mean, you know. I want to be liked, I want to be pleasant. That's why I make myself unpleasant, because it's too feminine to want to please, it's unhealthy. Are you yourself so damned pleasing, by the way? You look rather sloppy, for example. How about trying to be a little neater, a businessman ought to put up a good front. That one should need to teach you such elementary things, the very simplest sales techniques.

You can go now, Silberstein said and smiled, one hand in front of his mouth, here are a couple of tens, I'm not in the market for ideas today.

Asp took the money.

Sometimes I wonder which of us is the other's fool, he said, adding thanks and dropping a curtsy. But of course we don't need to worry ourselves about that.

He left. From outside he drummed a furious tattoo on the whitewashed window.

Silberstein jumped and then collapsed. And suddenly, before he could stop it, there was a shout inside him.

Why do I seek out humiliation?

It was so violent and so unexpected that at first he didn't understand that the crying out was inside him. He looked around to see if Asp was still there. But Asp had gone.

He was alone.

Why do I seek out humiliation?

Once again. He leapt up. I've got to get out of here, he thought, but stood still. Calm down, Silberstein, he said, just calm down, it's only a temporary relapse, it'll be over in a minute, it just came so suddenly that I didn't have time to defend myself.

His hands started shaking, sweat broke out on his forehead, it's the liquor, he thought, I have to stop drinking. He gripped the edge of the table, he tensed his whole body. Damned Asp, who is whose fool! He saw black, he was holding onto the table too hard, had to let go. His hands were still shaking.

I know very well why I seek out humiliation. The question needn't panic me. Then why does it shout so loud!

If there's anyone who'll look at me then I'll gladly dance for him so he can despise me all the more, if only he'll leave me in peace afterwards! I'm prepared to perform any trick, the audience can make a sacrament of these guilty pleasures.

As long as it's quiet.

As long as it's quiet! he screamed as loud as he could.

And now it was completely quiet inside him and around him.

He sat down, trembling, weariness relaxed him slowly, slowly. I don't suppose I'm about to go crazy, he whispered, is that the next danger? He sighed deeply. The sigh filled the room, touched the ceiling and walls, came back to him so that he breathed it in again.

Alone.

Relief.

He drew circles in the dust, his head leaning on one hand. His heart, which had pounded so violently, began to beat normally again. What happened, he thought, it can't be that I hate Asp, can it?

The thought made him frightened again, his heart raced, his hand trembled. He snorted. Why should I hate Asp? He's no concern of mine. No one is any concern of mine. It's because Asp can never be a concern of mine that I can socialize with him, have been spending what seems like many days and evenings with him, he performs great services for me, he helps me to renounce more and more, I use him; he, indeed, is my fool.

He kept on reasoning, but could find no peace. No more investigations now, he muttered, muttered again, chattered like an incantation, no more investigations now, but he couldn't make it credible, it sounded empty and distant. He searched for reasons but found only the liquor, the liquor, it's Asp who's maneuvered me into these alcoholic reflections, he thought, o indolence, o foolishness!

He started phoning – feverishly – but the results were poor, he hung up at the least resistance, even that first small resistance that was almost part of the ritual of greeting. He stormed through the list of numbers, even clients who'd heard from him just recently got a call. He himself could hear that he sounded more and more confused, no he had nothing new to offer, just wanted to keep in touch, for God's sake, surely there was nothing wrong with that, hell, he didn't suppose he was interrupting them, if they were in such a damned rush then they must need oceans of hair tonic and mountains of pomade. No he wasn't trying to be amusing, good-bye!

He slammed down the receiver. Next number! It'll be just as well if the whole lot of them go to the devil! Then Asp will have to search for money somewhere else!

What was that! Wasn't there drumming on the window again?

He ran to the door, outside and up the stairs, the street was deserted. He thought he heard Asp's horselaugh, but he knew it was only his imagination. He went down into his cellar, locked himself in. He took out his wallet and checked. Yes, he could go to the restaurant tonight too, could even pick up the tab, no problem.

He sat down heavily. It was as if he were brooding without brooding about anything in particular, just overcome by a spell of brooding. He listened, but it was still quiet, no one was calling, no one was drumming, no one was laughing. He whispered a few of Asp's invectives, listened, still quiet, it was over.

He put his ear to his wristwatch. Time was going – slowly.

What day could it be? He didn't know.

Time soon to sit across from Asp in the restaurant and grin ingratiatingly.

He took a piece of paper and began writing numbers. First numbers that had to do with the business, then numbers that didn't have to do with anything. They all looked equally ridiculous. He began doodling faces with the numbers, they were less abstract that way. He tried to do a self-portrait in numbers, that would no doubt be the height of objectivity, but it seemed he had forgotten what he looked like. His nose a backward six, his chin a backward three lying on its back, nothing but backward all the way – why exactly his right profile? Perhaps the best resemblance like that; what a way to do your accounts. What if he were to enter Asp in the books. Full-face bookkeeping. Zeros inscribed in a big zero. Even a little revenge is sweet.

But why revenge?

He grew uneasy again. What did he want revenge against Asp for? Asp who did nothing but perform services for him.

He ought to invite Asp up one night. Buy a half-liter and invite him up after the restaurant, not just leave him crying outside the entrance door.

He sat there making vague plans, knowing he didn't mean anything by them. Wouldn't dream of letting Asp inside his door – any more than anyone else. My home is my castle.

He continued drawing, filled a whole sheet of paper with eights. What for? Oh, nothing. Eights for exactly nothing. Best that way. A perfectly splendid number for nothing. A couple of zeros stacked up on each other. Hopeless and fine number.

Write. Writing games. We played writing games. Sara and I sat opposite each other at the big dining-room table and it was warm in the room and the whole table full of scribbled slips of paper . . .

The smell of a candle.

Where did the candle come from? Yes, Mammi used to light candles, just because it was cozy . . .

Hell and damn!

He threw the pen into the shelf full of jars. To sit here playing the fool and pretending to be moved. Disgusting. Just because the afternoon hours are slow as hell. It's time eating its way backward when it doesn't want to pass. It's the minutes that are sick, not me. The slowness hangs there sagging and spreading out, and memory switches on automatically. A robot on which you happen to finger a harmless switch. No worse than that. Absolutely not.

The minutes eat their way backward and forward. In a few hours he would be able to say, Now I'm sitting across from Asp, now I'm drinking. All he had to do was hurry over there ahead of time in his mind and then sit there and wait, and not let himself be disturbed by anything.

Did he really long to be there? He didn't long to be anywhere, waiting was a time-killer like all other time-killers.

Now I'm sitting across from Asp. Now I'm drinking.

He sat across from Asp. He drank.

Yes, you Jew-clown, there'll soon be an end to this damned boozing. At least for me. You can keep going under your own steam. I have a job that demands diligence, it's not just a matter of picking up a telephone receiver and raking in money. How the hell did the Jews manage before there were telephones. They had to run around, right? Got exercise and looked scrawny and aroused pity. Before the age of the telephone and obesity. You're not laughing very much this evening, Silversteen. Aren't I speaking crudely enough? You're rather fat and not particularly appetizing to have across the table when one is sitting in a posh restaurant and trying to enjoy the bounties of the board. Will that do? Grin a little, then. I'm not being paid very well for my services, so you can't expect too much. Besides, you make it hard for me, since I like you so damned much. But don't you think I understand what you're using me for! I'm supposed to sit here and be the court anti-Semite for you! It's a shitty job. I'm supposed to spit out all the taunts you're afraid of so they'll fade and become completely safe. They're supposed to chime in your ears like children's stories. O, to what base uses we may be turned, as Hamlet says.

Yes you're chuckling a little now, old man. To think that I should need to call on Shakespeare for help. But as a matter of fact you look terribly embarrassed. What's the matter with you? Aren't you completely shameless yet? Yes, I know you're a tactful person, very sensitive, and I'm not kidding, so you shouldn't have grinned just now. More whiskey!

The restaurant music shrilled, violinistic violins, the place hadn't begun to reel yet, it was as if the liquor had no effect on Silberstein tonight. Something was changing. He looked at this Asp who was supposed to say everything he was afraid of hearing so he wouldn't need to be afraid of it anymore. Asp looked tired, he's starting to get tired of me, thought Silberstein, I'm not a good audience anymore.

Are you starting to get tired of me, asked Asp.

Silberstein shook his head.

Yes indeed, you're starting to get tired of me, said Asp. You want coarser titillation than I can come up with, so I'll soon be thrown on the garbage-heap. Life is tough, right? But watch out, now! Perhaps it won't be as easy to find Judeophiles as you may think.

All at once he sounded threatening. His features acquired something that almost resembled sharpness. It showed in the corners of his mouth, and a couple of wrinkles appeared around the base of his nose.

You hate me, Silversteen, he said in a low voice, you're falling, how are you going to manage to get out of this now, hm?

Then he tilted his chair back and nonchalantly balanced on it. Jews, he said and neighed, you always think that you're damned well covered up and full of impenetrable complications, and now you're laid right out on the table. Would you like a few dirty words now? And he neighed again.

Silberstein ordered more whiskey. He sat there heavy and deflated. You're talking nonsense, boy, he said slowly.

Sure, said Asp lightly, you won't find a person in the whole world who'll claim otherwise.

Could it really be that I hate him, thought Silberstein – me, a worn-out old man. No, it can't be true.

The way you look, Asp laughed, you'd better watch out you don't swallow your nose, it seems to have gotten so damned long, and where have your beautiful eyes gone to. I think they've gone into your skull and disappeared. That's right, close your lids for a minute and see if you can find them.

Besides, I'm going somewhere else now. A female. I'd planned on letting her cool her heels tonight, but I got the urge. Have you noticed how the urge comes over you suddenly now and then? Have you got much of the urge left in you?

You'll pay, right?

And Asp got up and quickly walked straight out of the place, without turning around.

Do I hate him?

He left.

Come back, dear Asp!

You are a poison, a poison to be enjoyed. Masochism?

Asp a need? A guilty pleasure.

I've gone too far. I've gone too far.

I've got to get rid of Asp.

He called the waiter. He paid. His hands fumbled with his wallet. Suddenly people applauded. The music paused. He got up, a music-lover on his way out.

His hat far down over his eyes.

The world confronted him.

It seemed cold out.

9

You certainly saw a lot less of him now, he came home so late. Now and then you could hear someone shouting in the street at night, a drunken voice, it seemed that Silberstein had landed in bad company; surely this was disappointingly simple when you considered the interest you'd lavished on him in the beginning. But then, no one measures up in the long run, no one is worthy of your interest in people, as Olausson might say in a bitter moment, and who ever thanks you? No one. A bunch of flowers at the end of the term from some snot-nosed kid's mother who's worried about his grades, that's what you get for your interest in people and your efforts as a trainer of youth.

Silberstein's behavior pattern is all too common and simple.

More and more cringing in the morning. Why? Hung over.

Embarrassingly simple.

Out later and later at night. Why? Craving alcohol.

Boringly simple.

Olausson's expression suggested he felt distinctly wronged, or rather, slightly hurt as a sensitive human being. And that he was experienced. Knew a great deal about people.

Silberstein sloppier and coarser, greasier and slouch-hatty-er.

And that unnatural, irritating silence in the apartment. But just wait, soon came the stage when he would bring his drinking partners home, yelling, disturbances, smashed windows, vomit on the stairs. Well, to hell with him! At that point eviction was the only recourse. In the name of the social contract. No one can presume to be alone on earth.

To think that people could behave the way Silberstein would behave if he in fact ended up behaving that way!

Olausson shook his head.

Too often he'd seen the consequences: warped and intractable youngsters. Thank God Silberstein had no children. Now, on that score Silberstein's morality was irreproachable, that much you had to grant with a delicately ironic smile.

Humor.

Besides, Olausson wasn't the least interested in Silberstein. At present he had a rich inner life entirely on his own.

Had discovered that the name of the block, The Mirage, symbolized not only the housing shortage, but practically life itself.

Whether it was the poet in him that had given birth to the discovery or it was the discovery that had given birth to the poet was difficult to decide:

> We've enjoyed every winter that's come.
> We've delighted in summer's corsage.
> But oh how we know, every last one,
> that we live in this place: The Mirage.

He's a curious devil, that one, said Brundin, but at least he seems to booze like a human.

In the beginning I said he was the devil at making you curious, now I say he's a curious devil. Do you catch the nuances, old girl?

Have you seen his eyes? They're curious eyes. It's eyes like those that make you wish you could express yourself, make you wish you could describe things. If you don't have the gift of the gab, as it's called, usually you don't mind, but now and then you do.

Like when you're faced with the eyes on that Silberstein.

They're sad and kind behind the fear. You want to be decent. You always want to be decent. But when you see that curious devil's eyes, you wish you could really act on your decency.

You and your invitation to coffee! Dear girl, if only you didn't look as if you'd discovered a new breed of giant hog every time you make one of your suggestions. Oh yeah – so you don't think I'm doing much better when I say cognac too; well, I can assure you that coffee's much better with cognac.

But I don't think we should invite this particular fellow to anything at all.

They say that he's a Jew and it's clear that he's a Jew, and that's all there is to it.

But there's something about his eyes.

Seems to you I'm oversensitive, you say. Well, my girl, you sure can say the silliest things sometimes.

I met him on the stairs yesterday. Good day, I said, and he just tipped his hat, but that didn't make me angry one bit.

I make a point of saying good day, as a matter of courtesy, but this time it was oddly wrong. Not that he puts on airs.

But some people should be left in peace.

It's somehow good and fitting that certain people should be left in peace. I used to think it was wrong that certain people should be left in peace, but it isn't.

It's just fine that he lives in the building. It's nice to meet him on the stairs. It shouldn't go any further, though.

You and your coffee!

What would you say, looking straight into those eyes of his?

I'm just asking.

You wouldn't say a damned thing, and you'd be following the right instinct, dear girl.

Well, he's certainly not getting along very well. That much is easy to see. There's something wrong with him inside, and even if you had all the coffee in Brazil to offer. . . .

But it's actually nice to meet him on the stairs now and then. It shouldn't go any further than that.

Four storeys high on an otherwise empty lot, what was left of the block called The Mirage. The wreck stood there and would no doubt remain standing until whoever had to decide could figure out what the block would be used for.

Would probably happen suddenly, like most things in life.

The nameplates were still screwed on tight, including the one with the oddest name on the most beautiful plaque. Where the mailman never stopped, just swung quickly past.

The name, for that matter, wasn't so odd anymore. Slid over your tongue like other names, without raising a second thought, without starting you guessing its origin.

In fact it would have been almost odd if the man had been named anything else. Silberstein was Silberstein, anything else would have been strange and wrong. Pettersson or Graystone or Oleander – no, it would be just impossible. People and their names grow together, even if they're called the strangest things. Brundin's fat old lady was named Lillemor, there was nothing odd or funny about that just because it meant Little Mother. And she was childless besides. You never connected that with the name if you didn't reflect on it. Specifically, that is.

And that point about *shtine* and not *stine* had also sunk in. How in hell could you ever have thought it was *stine!* That sounded exactly as dumb as it was.

Surely you would have figured that out without Schoolmaster Olausson.

You never thought, either, about how the name was perhaps

rather pretty to belong to a fellow who was ugly as sin. There didn't seem to be any contradiction in that.

He belonged with his name, no question about it.

Perhaps belonged in the building too. All things considered. It just turns out that way. In the end, it feels right to have someone in the building who isn't right for it. That's what you call a charitable arrangement. A sort of getting accustomed. And custom becomes habit.

The unsuitable suits just fine. If only the tenant behaves in a suitably unsuitable way. Strictly speaking, this one doesn't behave at all – either well or poorly – but that'll probably become part of the building too, and will fit in.

Yes, Silberstein fits in here, you might say, however peculiar it sounds. Could you say why? No, you really couldn't. If you could, there would probably be something far-fetched about it, as in most explanations of things that get the way they are gradually instead of suddenly. For whatever's sudden there are always explanations. For the slow things it's more difficult, not to say impossible.

If you were to go up to that Silberstein and say to him: You fit in here, Mr. Silberstein, he would be truly surprised.

Even though he may never have thought otherwise.

But he would be surprised at your coming up to him and saying it, not at what you'd said but at your saying it; but then, he'd certainly be surprised in any event. The poor old guy.

What was peculiar was that you thought of how he fit in, that you told yourself that he fit in after all.

But of course he'd still only been there a short while.

Besides, who ever fits in anywhere, someone said.

Someone bitter.

Oh, the banging on the entrance door late at night made her feel so disappointed – that he came home so late, the poor man, and in such company, that drunken voice that sometimes shouted the most horrible things. She could never make out Mr. Silberstein's own voice, he was so discreet and subdued, that fine man, didn't want to disturb her or anyone else, that was clear. It's clear, thought Miss Svensson, that he's in a bad way, and in such company one is surely more lonely than if one were alone, Mr. Silberstein, there's so much that is beautiful in the world, so many lovely conversations are waiting behind my door.

She felt like biting on her sheet with the pretty monogram – out of sorrow and perhaps a touch of fear as well, imagine if he – no, not someone so discreet – but she herself had started up the acquaintance, after all, and when a man is inebriated you can never tell what he – no, not Mr. Silberstein, who knew what persecution and torment – but if nonetheless, how should she – with a warm voice and a friendly smile that would make him ashamed, and then the next day a big bouquet of roses – oh, my dear, dear Mr. Silberstein, there was no harm done and such beautiful flowers, so unnecessary, but thank you just the same, I love roses, they're my favorite flowers!

But she knew that he would never – no, of course not – that fine man, he would never ring her bell, and in the middle of the night! It was just her old maid's fear playing tricks on her, her girlish loneliness, and that light sleep that comes with the years, if it comes.

She lay tossing in her bed, feeling her heart beat. I'm so foolish, she sometimes thought, I'm so foolish and lonely, Mr. Silberstein is also lonely, won't I ever escape my silly fantasies. A silly old maid, hungry for company, how comical! She tried to laugh in the dark, bravely, old maids like me are supposed to be religious, knit sweaters for their relatives' babies, give discreet advice on refined reading matter, and never show any anxiety – only many thanks for your kind neglect and Christmas and New Years cards and one visit a year.

She would cry into her pillow – at her age! And when she had cried until she was calm she would lie there and consider Mr. Silberstein with a clear eye: how alien he was, and frightening and rather ugly to look at, and somehow a little bewitching and Grimmly menacing, oh Jesus was this what she called a clear eye!

I've read too many books. A fine confession coming from an old librarian!

Read aloud for him, since it's clear he's afraid of conversation.

I'm reading aloud for him in the dusk, I must finally be getting a bit sleepy, I'm reading aloud for him, he's getting up and coming closer, he's stroking my cheek with his hand, but why does he look as if he meant to hit me, I'm not hurting anyone, after all, and why is he laughing, I'm not reading poorly, and why is he leaning forward and kissing me on the forehead with that grimace, he's certainly no beauty either, besides which he smells of alcohol, I don't think he ever listens to a word I read, just sneers nastily when I have my eyes on the page.

Mr. Silberstein, go away!
I loathe him.
I have trouble sleeping.

Those who felt compassion for him because of the difficult things he had perhaps had to go through didn't feel compassion very long. They titillated themselves for a while with horror and disgust, but soon ended up in hollow repetition. Not that he showed any gratitude for the sympathy either. Not that they got a chance or had any especial desire to show their sympathy, but surely he had to do a little understanding from his side too. It's damned easy to just go around looking tragic and pleading. Besides, it was a long time now since those camps. Now there were reparations and compensation instead.

And of course they should have them, it's only right. But after that I'll be damned if it isn't time for them to stop sulking. Well, no, maybe sulking wasn't a very good expression to use about someone who had perhaps lost all his relatives, but you can't always be so exact about nuances. And besides, why should they always require the expense of so much nuance?

Though of course it was nice to feel a little sympathy now and then, a warm and comfortable feeling. You could almost get furious at him sometimes because he couldn't manage to keep your sympathy alive. And naturally that was unfair. It's so much trouble to be fair. He could really be rather troublesome, that Silberstein.

But how should he behave? Actually it was no small task you were setting him, you didn't quite know what it was, but it was big for sure. Inside yourself you were unfair when it came to him. He made you unfair, you realized you were being unreasonable, and then you got furious at him. Poor guy! Lucky for him that you saw through yourself. Otherwise you might be out and out dangerous for him.

That must be how it happened, you see. People became anti-Semites in just that way sometimes. It could be that complicated. Lucky you were on guard. Lucky for him to be among sensible, alert people. He'd been fortunate, in fact. Ought to be grateful to his good luck, if he couldn't be toward people, the ungrateful wretch. But maybe he was. Maybe he was very grateful, but had lost the ability to show it. After all, that would hardly be surprising.

You had to understand. If you couldn't manage to feel sympathy anymore, at least you had to understand. It seemed important. Understand him, but also yourself. It was like a discovery. What a fragile vessel one's decency is. It was a troubling but important discovery.

Though of course you knew that all along. You didn't really need him to come along and make it clear for you.

That's what you sensed: there was something pretentious about him!

After all, he wasn't one bit more important than any other human being. Each one has his fate to endure, we all have our fates, no doubt we all have a right to be pretentious if that's how it has to be.

Surely everyone has a right to sympathy. More or less, of course. Perhaps he had a right to more.

But in that case he could certainly say how things were and tell what had happened and not go around exacting a pound of sympathy that perhaps . . .

Was he exacting anything, in fact? No, but he surrounded himself with an aura that . . .

You ended up bearing him a grudge.

That's what you had to be on guard against, otherwise he would really deserve all that sympathy.

Should it be so easy to get over your compassion and so hard to get over your grudge?

And those who loved each other under his auspices? The ones who made their security glow against the background of his vulnerability?

They could still feel a wonderful benevolence toward him when they lay in each other's arms. Anxiously they kept alive the thought of his hard fate. And they were very humane as they lay there up close to each other. It seemed to them that their warmth was spreading over the world and they felt as if they were taking in the ugly old man and tenderly caressing him. They almost wept over their good feelings toward him. They let him chill them a bit so they could then enjoy each other's warmth, and the warmth grew so strong that they could send some of it out to him through the dark night. They felt this way even when they heard him fumbling with his keys and then huffing and puffing on the stairs, and were disgusted by his decay. At these moments the young man, vigorous and full of initiative, felt splendid. The young woman felt a delicious need to cry. Everything became so sweet and rosy.

I always smile at him, she said, and can you imagine – it's as if he didn't notice, isn't that awful?

You smile at everyone, he said.

Don't tell me you're jealous of old Silberstein, she said, scratching him on the chest, and he'd cut his first widdle baby-toof of jealousy, and the whole thing was very sweet and old Silberstein was surprisingly useful, he was really an asset for romance.

He puts some color into life, she said.

My precious, he said, knowing more about life than he wanted to say; he knew of course about the wars and all the human wreckage they'd left, but she might as well stay on her little planet that spread such delightful warmth and supported his vigor and his initiative so perfectly.

Do you think he's ever had a woman, she whispered coyly, using Silberstein to show how well off people were who had women and homes and food on the table and the bed all made and someone in the made-up bed and who thanks to all this could display vigor and initiative.

You're like a child, he said and hugged her, not having understood a thing.

I don't think you understand how pitiful Silberstein is, she persisted.

Sweet child, don't try to venture into politics, he laughed tenderly.

Politics, she said, and felt dumb and therefore a little angry. I'm sure it has nothing to do with politics.

I said you shouldn't try, didn't I, he huffed. You don't understand politics, and it's best that way.

She felt that she was angry at Silberstein.

I don't give a damn about him or politics or you either, she sulked.

He was charmed and hugged her tight. My precious, he said, don't you know you're the only thing I care about! Silberstein's certainly nothing to quarrel about.

Have we quarreled, she asked happily. I'm so stupid. You see everything in a broader perspective than I do. I smile at the old Jew and you place him in larger contexts, that's the difference between us.

That's the difference between men and women, he said contentedly. How soft you are.

You never answered my question, she whispered.

What question?

Whether you thought that Silberstein had ever had a woman.

You silly, he said, and kissed her.

And she felt that she wasn't angry at Silberstein anymore.

Yes, you saw less of him now, perhaps heard him a bit more, this business at night.

Renkvist, the journalist, who also kept late hours, unlocked the entrance door for him one night, and he was obviously embarrassed about the loudmouth who was with him and who kept begging and pleading to be allowed up.

I hope you didn't hesitate on my account, said Renkvist, no one in the building makes a fuss if someone has overnight guests.

But Silberstein just shook his head, tipped his hat, and puffed his way up the stairs a little faster than he could really manage, Renkvist stepping lightly beside him, teasing his shyness a trifle.

Besides which, we shouldn't give a good goddamn what people think – as long as we don't break the law: these days it's not easy to find a new apartment.

But no answer.

But it's enough, after all, to worry without quite crossing over into panic, persisted Renkvist. Isn't that right, Mr. Silberstein?

No answer.

We too have late guests now and then, hope we don't disturb you, you seem to be very particular about silence, continued Renkvist, his tone now more sharply ironic.

Still no answer. Just off with his hat again, jingling of keys, deep sigh, typical bore, one hell of a moper.

Good night, Mr. Silberstein.

Quiet in the stairwell.

Impossible to judge the degree of intoxication, said Renkvist to his wife. Doesn't weave when he walks, but doesn't dare to open his trap.

How about your own degree, asked Mrs. Renkvist sleepily.

Healthy and fine and moderate, said Renkvist. Balance medium. Fluency medium. Medium straight down the line. I'm a very medium person.

He looks tired, said Mrs. Renkvist.

Do you see him often?

See him now, answered Mrs. Renkvist. Can see him in front of me. He looks tired. Shouldn't stay up so late. Shouldn't invite so many questions. The questions buzzing all around him are tiring him out.

You don't say. Well it happens, said Renkvist, that people ask less about him now than in the beginning.

It's more than enough, said Mrs. Renkvist. The buzzing around him is wearisome. And I guess you contributed your two cents tonight too.

Yes, I gave a little buzz, Renkvist admitted. I don't approve of silence.

Right now he looks like a big, tired dog, said Mrs. Renkvist.

More like a sea lion, said Renkvist.

Don't make fun of me.

I'm just buzzing a little.

He won't hold out very long, said Mrs. Renkvist. I can't tell by looking at him exactly how long he'll manage to hold out.

You seem pretty sleepy yourself, said Renkvist.

I'm very sleepy, said Mrs. Renkvist. I wonder if he falls asleep fast. I hardly think so.

And the children, the lovable little ones?

All the little thumb-suckers who bow and curtsy so nicely. And all the boisterous boys and all the blue-eyed folksong lassies in belled skirts who whisper their secrets on the street corner.

They sensed the uncertainty surrounding him, both from him and from others, their parents and the other grown-ups.

Hi, old Jew!

There was no harm in it, after all. Just looked as if he hadn't heard it.

You get any booze yesterday?

It was all right to shout that, because Mama had said . . . Though Papa said that it was nobody's business.

Drew a swastika on his door. Always fun to scrawl things in the stairway.

Renkvist, the journalist, saw it, got furious, chased us away, wiped it off. What made it any of his business, huh? No drawing allowed in the stairway, of course. But Renkvist used to be okay.

Morning, Moses. Hello, Abraham.

Great. Actually looked a little scared. Didn't turn around.

A few of these sniveling missies would curtsy to him. But they were never allowed to do anything, so you couldn't expect very much.

Do you have anything against him, Renkvist asked, looking curious about it.

Course not, why should we? What a question!

Hi there, Yid.

Brundin heard that, raised his fist and galloped after us, panting – out of shape.

Well, isn't he a Yid?

Why was there always such a fuss about him, anyway? What made him a little menacing? Because that's what he was for sure, you could feel it from the grown-ups.

Besides which, it was the grown-ups who'd sent you out on little missions to sniff out what the old guy really did all day.

Looked like a boring job, and looked like it didn't pay off very good.

Jar-job.

Kolla chalked a great drawing in the entranceway. Hook nose

dipped deep in a jar. And next to that the same snout with grease on it.

But those didn't stay there long either.

That was definitely one gloomy old guy. Never bothered to smile at children, the way you should. Had no manners.

Mama agreed with that.

The Red Sea never should have let them through, one guy said. Terrific. Must have picked it up in school.

Have you gone down and thanked the Red Sea, Israel?

No go, not a flicker. No sense of humor.

You could get awfully tired of him.

Long live Jesus!

Actually came home alone these nights. Nobody shouting outside the building or crying under the streetlamp. Just alone and worn out.

His friend must have gotten tired of him. At any rate, the festivities never moved into the apartment the way Olausson had predicted. It seemed the schoolmaster needed to re-examine his knowledge of human beings.

But the entrance door banged harder, the puffing got worse, and he wasn't so careful with his apartment door either. It would echo in the stairwell. In fact he made noise inside the apartment too, that was something new, must be getting even drunker now. Things like that accelerate, everyone knows how that works. A couple of glasses the first time, then it's a brook, a stream, a river, a lake, an ocean. And then of course you know what happens.

But more solitary, more of an oddball than ever.

Someone had seen him alone in a pub way downtown. Sitting and rocking in time to the music and grinning stupidly with worm-eaten teeth. Ridiculously polite to the staff, almost fawning. Staggered out, almost. Nearly an awkward situation. But we didn't greet each other, after all, so no one noticed we were acquainted. Some acquaintance. No one really knows him, even though he's lived here for a while now. Then too, you have to be on your guard with people who go drinking alone. He could just as well bring the stuff home instead, would be cheaper, but he must have been able to afford it, had probably palmed off a lot of jars lately.

Someone else had seen him in another pub.

So: grand rounds.

And alone everywhere. No more pal.

Really needed a pal. To lean on. Could hear him stumbling on the stairs.

And yet – up earlier and earlier in the morning. Obviously slept badly. Sometimes out at the same time as the school kids. Some of them yelled stupid things at him, but what could you do about it – not much aside from having a word with them. For that matter he could tell them off himself, but it seemed as if he didn't care, maybe he couldn't hear for the drunken rush in his ears and the surge of the headache in his skull; after all, that early in the morning there wasn't room for anything but the hangover's hammer and anvil.

Miserable.

There's no question that misery arouses a certain sympathy. You can feel you're being rather splendid. It was nice to have that fresh taste in your mouth when you happened to catch sight of him some morning.

But he burdened the walls with sighs. You could hear his sighs through the double floors. At night, if you couldn't sleep. Or so it might seem.

Aside from that no one heard him at all.

When you saw him you might think: time keeps passing to no purpose and every day has the same color.

He was like an image of hopelessness and it was hard to shake him off.

Unsteadier than usual tonight.

Renkvist followed him to the entrance door at a reasonable distance, whistling to himself; Silberstein held onto the lamppost, risked letting go of it, a couple of sideways steps, a couple in the right direction. Then he was there.

No, old boy, tonight you're going to have to fumble until you get your own keys out!

Renkvist stood waiting behind Silberstein, whistling nonchalantly, sensing with delight that he was making him nervous.

There – so he managed it in the end.

No, after you, Mr. Silberstein, do please – oh, thanks very much.

Silberstein stopped in the entranceway and propped himself up against the wall, obviously waiting for Renkvist to go by.

We can keep each other company on the way up, Mr. Silberstein. Renkvist stayed where he was, mocking.

The old man under way, without a word, as usual. Renkvist beside him, exaggeratedly sociable.

The whirl of entertainment and the temptations of the social life, ah yes, Mr. Silberstein.

Panting heavily.

Here, take my arm, between that and the banister you'll get to your door easily; liquor is such a traitor.

Quickened his pace, puffed even more, didn't take the arm.

You couldn't see the old man's face, head down, hat with the wide brim.

I'm hunting him, thought Renkvist. I guess I'm not being very nice. But damn me if he isn't going to learn to answer. To show some ordinary manners.

Stumbled, caught himself with his hand, that was almost a pratfall, that one.

One must learn to accept help, Mr. Silberstein.

I'll be damned if the old boy didn't try to take two steps at once, that'll never work.

You see! Stumbled again. Was too eager now, near his door, both hands on the landing, looked too funny on all fours like that.

But if he doesn't want any help he isn't going to get any.

Stayed in that position a ridiculously long time. Renkvist next to him, waiting. Then he turned around clumsily and just sat down on the stairs. Sat there.

Suddenly looked up at Renkvist.

A strange, a disturbing look. Renkvist suddenly weak in the knees.

What am I up to?

The look very reproachful, and a lot else in it besides, altogether too much.

Renkvist had to sit down as well. Sat down next to him. In the stairwell, in the small hours, in the drab stairway light.

My wife says that you must be very tired, said Renkvist helplessly.

And the first answer, his head lowering again, his hands fumbling with his coat.

I am very tired.

I am very tired, said Mr. Silberstein.

He set his palms on the stairs as if he were thinking of getting up again, but gave up. Head lowered.

You must think that I'm terribly drunk.

I thought so but I'm changing my mind, said Renkvist.

I am terribly drunk, said Silberstein, but that doesn't matter. That's not what matters.

What is it that matters, asked Renkvist.

Aha, said Silberstein, you too! You too are a philosopher.

Renkvist somewhat offended. Sooner drunk than a philosopher, he said. I have no great respect for philosophers. Besides, philosophers these days aren't what they used to be.

No, I'm sure they aren't, said Silberstein. You are indeed right as far as that goes.

His head still lowered. Renkvist couldn't tell whether or not he was being ironic. Silberstein's tone was completely neutral.

The timer-switch turned off the stairway light.

Silberstein's breathing in the dark. Not moving. Renkvist got up, groped for the switch, found it and turned the light on. Silberstein in the same position. Renkvist sat down next to him again.

I feel like talking, said Renkvist. Silberstein sighed heavily. Silence.

I feel like talking, repeated Renkvist.

I heard you, said Silberstein. Talk!

Renkvist laughed. That was some invitation, he said. Nighttime, the stairwell, it's splendid. It's on such occasions one talks about life.

Life is moods, said Silberstein.

Yes, said Renkvist. That and much else. One can say "Life is" and then finish it in every conceivable way and nowadays everything sounds equally fine and plausible.

No, said Silberstein, no it doesn't. You're mistaken.

Silberstein set his elbows on his knees and supported his heavy head. Some light shone on his face. His face had no expression. The expressionlessness was frightening, a completely empty nakedness, the eyelids heavy, the mouth half open. You could read into that face anything you cared to. Renkvist read in pain.

Where do you come from, Mr. Silberstein?

Silberstein snorted. Now you're being philosophical again, he said.

Not at all, said Renkvist. I mean exactly what I'm asking.

Don't the philosophers too, asked Silberstein.

Renkvist decided to laugh. He laughed.

You laugh, said Silberstein. Your question was perhaps not philosophical but psychological. You think I behave in a certain way and now you want to have the background. Where do you come from? That's a completely irrelevant question. Life is moods. It makes absolutely no difference where I come from.

I don't believe it, said Renkvist.

There are many people who come from the same place as I do. We are all very different.

Renkvist became irritated.

We are all very different, repeated Silberstein. Origin, qualities – oh God, don't go making me into some character in a novel!

He rocked back and forth.

I don't have the slightest desire to arouse curiosity, he said. I've freed myself of all coquetry long ago. I hang out no shingle, I've dissolved what could be called my character, life is just moods.

You're repeating yourself, said Renkvist.

That's all right with me, said Silberstein. In your head you have a set of books where you keep track of acquaintances, you enter character traits and record types, I'm sure you have an excellent and very appropriate system. Don't trouble yourself about me, I don't belong there, I can't be catalogued.

That's vanity, said Renkvist.

You're slapping on labels, Silberstein muttered. What a party game! Where do you come from? What a question!

I'm a journalist, said Renkvist. I'm experienced at asking questions. I ask them well. I have a passion for my work.

I'm sure, said Silberstein. And I do everything I can to avoid being in the newspapers.

Not a flicker. Not a smile. Chin in hands, gaze straight ahead or lowered and hidden under his eyelids.

No, you're no subject for an interview, said Renkvist. You don't excite my professional instincts. But without being intrusive, I'd like to say that there is something affecting about your person, something . . .

So, said Silberstein curtly.

Without being intrusive . . .

You are intrusive.

Renkvist decided to laugh. I'm laughing out of pity, he thought; that's unusual. I'm laughing instead of getting angry. I definitely pity the old man.

You are assigning qualities to me, continued Silberstein. I would simply like to inform you that I have no qualities. I have freed myself of coquetry. In this way I have come to be of no concern to anyone. I am no concern of yours, and that's just fine.

Why, asked Renkvist; why is that just fine?

Silberstein let out a short, hoarse laugh.

You think you've got me now, he said, but that's a mistake. Because a person free of coquetry can never be provoked into answering.

You're not easy to make conversation with, said Renkvist.

Because I'm not in the mood, said Silberstein.

And life is moods, said Renkvist. I've heard that before.

But you most likely haven't understood it, said Silberstein. Most likely not. You don't need to understand it, either. You have other knowledge. Good knowledge, I'm sure. Certainly very useful knowledge.

His voice was very clear, without a trace of irony, sooner with a touch of envy, thought Renkvist. Perhaps he was envious?

No, I am not envious, said Silberstein all of a sudden; I believe I am free of envy too. I don't say so to boast, quite the contrary, for if life is precious, which I naturally doubt, then all envy is healthy, in fact positive and vital. Not for me, then. Furthermore I'm talking too much.

Perhaps you've gotten into the mood, said Renkvist.

Probably. I'm usually careful, but since it's a habit and not a character trait, my carefulness works loose rather easily. It isn't rooted in a character; and that ought to make me careful and get me to say good night.

Do you know, by the way, why I'm usually careful?

Because you're a Jew?

Good God, no. Because I'm usually afraid. It's that simple. You see, everything about me is much simpler than you've imagined.

Now he sounded almost cheerful.

Afraid because I'm a Jew! The Jews I've known who have succeeded in keeping their qualities intact have generally been virtually heroic. Among Jews with qualities, courage is quite common.

I've read about that, said Renkvist.

You are no doubt very well read, said Silberstein. If everyone were as well read as you, perhaps I would be less afraid.

Now he sounded clearly ironic. Renkvist got up and turned on the light, which had gone out again.

I too am often afraid, said Renkvist. I don't think it's especially remarkable.

No, it's courage that's remarkable, said Silberstein, I've never thought otherwise. For a fearful person, courage has to be decidedly more interesting than fear. Just as trust is more interesting than suspicion.

One can't live in a continual state of suspicion and fear, it's a humiliation, said Renkvist.

You are wrong and you are right, said Silberstein. One certainly can live in a state of fear and suspicion, and this certainly is a humiliation. One just mustn't think too badly of humiliation – it's a possibility.

What is one left with in that case, asked Renkvist.

Life, said Silberstein.

Renkvist laughed again. Good God, how pathetic you are, he said. And sentimental.

Silberstein shook it off. Labels again, he muttered, if only it were that simple! As if humiliation didn't need to be conquered, along with everything else! Just as much as all other religions.

Free yourself of qualities, conquer humiliation – you certainly have ambitions there, said Renkvist.

I have nothing, insisted Silberstein, and it's a good thing. The other day one of the kids shouted at me that I ought to go down and thank the Red Sea. Naturally in many respects it was a proper recommendation, which I am not going to follow. I thought of my forefathers who had seen the enormous, terrifying walls of water, who had walked that path of fear on the floor of the world and who then stood safe on the other shore and were supposed to be grateful. I wondered whether they had any qualities left. Whether they hadn't in fact been obliterated. I think there was an enormous silence on the shore, a silence that amazed the Lord, until someone struck up the usual song of praise in order to fill the astonishing void within him, and the prophetess Miriam and all the women began to dance and beat their timbrels to break the dreadful stillness and silence of nothingness. For it is wrong to think that you get purified and strengthened by walking dry-shod through the Red Sea, you stand there gaping on the shore and the tremendous wave drowns what you call your character and your qualities, and then you stagger onward through a desert, and the Lord can go right ahead and make it rain manna, you dance around the golden calf just the same with your heart pounding in the void and your life trickling away.

The Lord could have built a bridge instead – that would have been a more merciful miracle!

He fell silent. He was panting, as after a great physical effort, and perhaps his speaking had been that too. Renkvist was ill at ease. Hell of a mood-weaver, he thought, now he's got me in his spell. No qualities, no coquetry! And then to perform like an old stage whore. Damned timer, now it was dark again.

He got up and pushed the button. God's eye is winking at you, Mr. Silberstein, he thinks your reading of his Bible is devilishly clever, he's been caught completely off guard, and now he's ashamed, isn't he, Mr. Silberstein?

I don't care about him, said Silberstein calmly. There are some people who can't experience humiliation without establishing a relationship with God. As for me, he doesn't interest me. We abandoned each other long ago without any fuss, and parted with an exchange of polite phrases. I do talk to him sometimes, but it's a sort of game you can easily play with anything that doesn't exist. Why should I begrudge myself that? It gives your natural talkativeness an outlet and you don't go striking up an acquaintance with just anybody.

Thanks, said Renkvist. That means there's God and me.

I'm afraid not, said Silberstein. I've fallen on several other occasions. My way of using God is of course complete sacrilege, as you can see, but it's not the solemn type, it's plain laziness. Both are equally unforgivable from a religious point of view; that is, if anything is unforgivable from a religious point of view – there are such different teachings about that on the market.

You're a humanist, I suppose?

Why do you ask, said Renkvist, that came a bit abruptly.

I must, after all, be unforgivable from a humanistic point of view as well, said Silberstein. No one can claim that I'm fighting for human dignity. I'm not fighting at all. That must mean I'm atrocious.

I'm not going to accuse you of anything, said Renkvist. I'm not thinking of lecturing you on morality. I'm not at your service.

Silberstein gave him a look, searching and perhaps somewhat embarrassed. Now you've caught me out, he said. You're right. I have a hard time passing up those tricks. It troubles me. It's not consistent with me.

Does everything have to be consistent?

Yes, sighed Silberstein, everything has to be consistent.

Even when one has freed oneself of all qualities?

Even then, said Silberstein, one must protect one's absence of qualities. Don't you think I notice that you're pitying me? Your pity is a strong temptation. I could easily paste on a few appealing qualities so I could relish you. I would grow uncertain, I would surrender myself to illusions of personality. I don't have what people call a personality. I don't want to have one.

For God's sake, don't pity me!

He had raised his voice, he was almost shouting in the stairwell. Renkvist hushed him and Silberstein crumpled up as if he'd been taken by surprise. They both sat listening for a while, but they heard nothing, the building was completely quiet. Silberstein made a motion as if to get up, Renkvist laid his hand on his arm and they remained sitting as they were. It seemed to Renkvist there was a rushing in his ears, he didn't know if it was fatigue or agitation, he felt that he was peculiarly agitated – I don't matter to him, he thought, why does one always want to matter, this greed that one calls helpfulness! Leave him in peace now, that's all he wants. Why can't one ever accept that attitude?

Whether or not I pity you is my affair, said Renkvist. There are limits to the consideration you have a right to expect. Furthermore your egocentricity is overbearing. You force a person to take a position.

Silberstein shot to his feet. For God's sake, he screamed, don't say that! I have nothing to do with anyone! Leave me in peace! The most dangerous thing in the world is to have something to do with someone!

His voice fell to a whine.

Why should you frighten me like this? Why do you have to be nasty to me? I haven't asked to talk with you.

You're waking the whole building, said Renkvist. Sit down! He took hold of Silberstein's arm and pulled, Silberstein plumped down heavily onto the stairs. Sorry, said Renkvist, did you hurt yourself?

Silberstein didn't answer. He sat there rocking back and forth again, with his arms folded over his stomach, as if he were nursing a great hurt. He mumbled something that Renkvist couldn't catch, maybe it wasn't even real words. Renkvist's anxiety mounted and became painful.

You are pitiful, he said.

Label again, muttered Silberstein. Let up!

There was a time when I wanted to be brave, he continued in the same voice as before, as if he were talking to himself – but I couldn't manage it; therefore I thought it best to become a Jew completely without qualities.

That's what I thought, and I was right. I was truly right. And I succeeded. The brave ones. I no longer admire them. I haven't even got my admiration left. I have nothing left. And it's best that way.

You run on too much to be credible, said Renkvist. I don't know whether it's me or yourself you're trying to convince.

I'm not trying to convince anyone, said Silberstein. I don't care about you. And I don't understand why you're hurt by that. I don't understand how it is that I can hurt anyone at all. I'm meaningless, after all, I don't matter in the least.

His tone quite dry.

The light again.

He's still sitting there, at any rate, thought Renkvist. If he really meant what he said he would have gone in and gone to bed a long time ago.

I can tell that you're wondering why I haven't gone in, said Silberstein. Don't think it's anything but the law of inertia and the longing for company that liquor gives a person. I'm not unsure of myself.

Suddenly he grinned. When you're sitting here, he asked, do you see me as an image of the Jew or the Human Being, Mr. Journalist? Oh, you with your little oilcloth-covered notebook inside you, what clear thoughts you must have about me!

Renkvist got mad. I'm thinking about myself, he said – it's catchy. I'm thinking about what you see me as an image of. It's certainly something damned foolish. Moods and qualities, those are your key words. Do you think that other people's souls have any more definite outlines. You've gone and brooded your way into stupidities and misunderstandings, Mr. Silberstein.

You said you were thinking about yourself, said Silberstein.

His tone still completely dry.

I am, said Renkvist, and I'll be damned if it isn't more enjoyable than thinking about you. You're boring. Human beings are mirrors, and since I've managed to stay interested, I reflect something other than myself and therefore present an image that's a bit more varied than yours.

Tell me about it, said Silberstein.

You wouldn't listen, said Renkvist. That's part of your program too, no doubt. Don't hear. Don't see. You must be awfully bored.

I am, said Silberstein.

Beyond reach.

I'm going to tell you a little about myself anyway, said Renkvist. Yes, go ahead and sigh, go in and go to bed if you don't want to listen. I am a journalist, you know that already, I'm good at it but I don't carry any weight. I have a smart and kind wife and we've become very attached to each other, as people do after a good number of years together. I quarrel with her when I feel like quarreling, I'm friendly to her when I feel like being friendly. I have a fair number of friends. I'm commonly considered a so-called regular guy.

I help old ladies across the street, I'm a courteous driver, I pay my taxes without grumbling, I'm as generous as the next fellow, I never mistreat animals, I don't hold many grudges, I get furious with kids when they set traps for small birds. But it is quite obvious that I am inclined to dislike Jews.

Silberstein's thick lower lip twitched but he said nothing. Renkvist considered the curving profile for a moment before continuing.

I haven't had any bad experiences. I consider myself impervious to crude propaganda. I know a few Jews. I have a decidedly high opinion of most of them. I don't like name-calling. I defend them when the occasion arises – backstabbing remarks dropped when none of them are around. But I am quite obviously inclined to dislike Jews.

He regarded Silberstein again. Silberstein sat there silent and motionless, but he had turned his head slightly, his glance was averted.

When one of them behaves badly I take it as a confirmation of my suspicions, said Renkvist.

That's too simple, muttered Silberstein, that's too simple.

When one of them behaves badly I think it's to be expected, said Renkvist. When one of you does something.

That's too simple, muttered Silberstein again. That's too simple a trick to get at me with.

I'm not up to any tricks, said Renkvist. I'm telling you how it is.

You're pressing me, said Silberstein. You're cruel.

I'm a regular guy, said Renkvist lightly.

My fear, said Silberstein. You want to give me a gigantic responsibility for my fear. You want to make my way of living have enormous consequences. You want to knock me to the ground because I'm not likable. You want to force me to have qualities.

Not everyone has the same inclination I do, you know, said Renkvist in the same light tone.

But enough of them do, said Silberstein.

What do you mean by enough, asked Renkvist.

Enough to give me that gigantic responsibility, said Silberstein. Enough to force me to provide myself with appealing qualities.

The light.

Renkvist switched it on.

Silberstein was still turned away. He maintained an unnatural stillness. Closed in on himself. Helplessly isolated, thought Renkvist.

Why do you say so, asked Renkvist. You wouldn't hurt a fly, after all.

No, said Silberstein, I don't take part in the great fly-hunt. I keep still. I stay away from everything. But my fear – my unappealing fear is reason enough.

Is it so unappealing?

Yes, for anyone who shares your inclination.

His voice very quiet.

It's a curse, he added. I wanted it to fall only on my own shoulders. We never escape.

Now you said "we" nonetheless, said Renkvist.

I never go to the synagogue, said Silberstein. I don't know anyone in the congregation. I have no family. My relatives are gone. It seems I have to say "we" nonetheless.

His voice very tired.

Renkvist felt a sort of triumph that he himself disliked. What have I gotten started on, he thought, what sort of shameful work am I carrying out in the night? Fly-hunt, manhunt. I never mistreat animals. One shouldn't speak too soon.

Forgive me, he said.

Silberstein grimaced. I won't permit it, he said vehemently, I won't permit you to ask me for forgiveness! I won't permit such clammy intimacies!

Then a frightened shudder.

I don't mean anything by it, he muttered, don't take me literally.

Forget the whole thing!

He got up heavily. Took hold of the banister and turned around.

Forget me, he said.

He scrounged awkwardly in his pockets, dug out his keys, rattled them, remained standing on the top step, hesitant. Renkvist considered him from below – the unpolished shoes, the rumpled clothing, the large ugly face under the broad-brimmed hat. He looks surprisingly monumental, he thought, it's astounding for someone so lost. There's not a bit of dignity in what he says, and yet . . . no, I'm sentimentalizing him, or maybe dramatizing, I don't know. I've always thought that the Jews have something ancient in them that frightens you or excites your imagination, or makes you romantic or hostile or whichever way you're affected, but maybe it's something immediate, the eternal or the immediately current, I don't know, I'm drunk, my brain is jelly. As a matter of fact I'm not drunk, I'm just trying to come up with a not overly painful explanation of my intellectual confusion. I'll be damned if I'm not sitting here feeling a little ashamed of myself.

Forget me, Silberstein muttered, and rattled his keys, and again that voice as if no one were there.

Ah yes, merciful forgetfulness, said Renkvist, it's always so comfortable, so soft to lie back on.

But it's hard to ask for, mumbled Silberstein. We're all afflicted with a strong desire to be remembered. It's one of the strangest temptations. Someone must remember me – what a peculiar desire! The final fear and the final prayer – don't forget me! Don't forget me, Emanuel! No, Papsi, no, Mammi, no, Sara, I promise . . . I'm the only one who's forced himself to ask for the opposite. I have practiced wanting to be forgotten. It's an art that hasn't been easy to master.

He remained standing there, rocking back and forth on the top step. Silent for a moment.

And every time I talk with someone the bell goes off somewhere inside me: remember me, think of me! No matter who it is. You, whoever you are. What whorishness! Of the many curses of loneliness, one of the hardest to conquer.

Hardest to conquer! I'm talking like a soldier. Me! That's really funny. Why aren't you laughing? Conquered or unconquered. Me! That shows I can't express myself properly.

As if I were waging some sort of battle. That's just what I'm not doing, after all. That's just what I don't want to do. A battle for oblivion. Now, there's a conquest to make! I who don't even have my self-contempt anymore.

Don't you, asked Renkvist.

Haven't I told you that I don't have anything left at all, said Silberstein. I've said that I've freed myself of coquetry and qualities. And nevertheless. What can I want anyone to remember in that case? It's absurd.

It's not always the person one remembers, though, said Renkvist. It can be his fate.

I haven't acquired any fate, said Silberstein. I have no expectations in that department.

Renkvist felt irritated. You are no one, you have no expectations, you have no fate. Who the hell am I talking to, actually? A nothing who says "Forget me" in order to be remembered. If you don't mind my saying so, Mr. Silberstein, what bullshit! If you have no other qualities then you have at least this one: that you've gotten stuck right up to your ass. That too can certainly be called a fate. Just don't think it's so damned remarkable that it can't be described with our most ordinary homespun words! Despite what you say, you're extraordinarily easy to sum up in a formula. A five-line item would do, I swear to God! Turn on the light.

Silberstein turned it on.

I don't want to be in an item, he said.

Don't worry, said Renkvist, we don't have that much extra space to fill – you have no value as news.

That's fine, said Silberstein. That's how I want it.

Sure, sure, said Renkvist, I know, I know. Enjoy your success! I don't understand why I keep sitting here and talking to you. It must be because I have the desire of a decent person to get control of my shameful inclinations. You can rest content. I'm talking to you purely out of interest in myself. Go in and go to bed and sleep with an easy mind!

You really go at it, said Silberstein calmly.

Yes I do, said Renkvist. I work in a profession where you rush around in the milling crowds. You develop a certain interest in everyone and everything. You get involved. You see different people and milieus and you try as best you can to tell about which ones are doing all right and which ones are doing badly. People talk a lot of crap about journalists. Almost all the ones I know have some kind of idealism. And you get in the habit of expecting that people and the things that happen to them will make you either glad or indignant.

I can only say that you mess it all up in a damned annoying way!

That wasn't a very good explanation, thought Renkvist. I can't get any of it to line up with this old man here. I'd better go to bed.

He got up. What am I doing, he thought. I'm defending myself. Why am I doing it? Why do I experience the old man as an accusation? It can't very well be – can it – for the sake of my neat little anti-Semitism, which I use as a demonic flourish in my exceedingly sleek spiritual life, and which I can't even take seriously myself.

Why do some people think they have a right to go around like living accusations against mankind? I want to escape. I'll go to bed.

Good night, Mr. Silberstein, he said.

Silberstein stood leaning against the wall. He was chewing as if he were about to say something, but no sound came out. On the other hand he didn't look like he was thinking of going either.

Renkvist's irritation mounted. I said good night, Mr. Silberstein, he said.

I've irritated you, said Silberstein slowly; it was unavoidable. If only you hadn't forced yourself on me. This eternal reprise. . . .

You see, where I lived before, the building was better than this one, the apartments were better. The people living in that building were very friendly, they were determined to be friendly, they had friendliness as their platform, you might say. I really didn't belong there.

I've had a hard time with friendliness, because I've seen friendliness change in a frightening way . . .

But I don't expect to belong, so I went on living there.

People in the building invited me to their places. I always

declined. They gave me friendly smiles. I smiled back as best I could.

There was one man there who was more determined to carry out the friendliness program than all the others. He was a leader type. From time to time he launched friendliness campaigns. He ran around calling people by their first names and handing out leaflets. During these periods all the neighbors visited each other even more eagerly than before, the whole building clinked with the sound of cups being set on saucers and all the grins got broader, the smiles looked almost savage. They all gave each other bear hugs. The friendliness-director looked very pleased. They all forgot to buy sugar so they could run to a neighbor and borrow some. That's how the whole building ended up without sugar one Sunday. By Monday there was a year's supply on hand. But little mishaps of friendliness like that were nothing to worry about.

I sneaked out of it all as best I could.

But the leader waylaid me.

One morning he was standing there right on the stairs. I couldn't get by. He winked at me. Then he quickly put a big button on my coat. A button with a terribly long pin. "First names!" said the button.

I didn't dare to take it off. After all, I might run into one of the friendlies. I was afraid someone would talk to me. Kept to myself.

One morning, there he stood again, legs wide apart, smile wide open. Brother, he said, hi there! He fastened a new button on my coat, with an even longer pin, next to the other one. "Be an optimist!" it said on the button.

The stairway light went out. Silberstein turned it on.

Yes, there I was, he continued, going in and out of the building with my buttons on my coat, trying to avoid being talked to, and looking pessimistic. The Minister for Friendliness shook his head, worried but smiling, whenever he met me. His "Hi there, brother" took on a more and more threatening tone. The others' keen nods became more and more exaggerated until they were macabre.

The leadership genius again. Friendliness Week now, he said, hi there and clap on the back. It's going to be a week of real celebration here. The friendly building! Wash your windows, brush your teeth, smile at your neighbor!

I shut myself in and pulled down the shades.

For a whole week I lived on canned food and only took my fingers out of my ears to open cans. There was music coming from all the apartments, it combined into a frightening cacophony in my rooms. They danced so the ceiling lamps shook. The telephone rang continuously, the doorbell rang, people banged on the door, brochures came dancing in through the mail slot – guides to the art of being friendly.

When Friendliness Week was over I was visited by an inspector from the Board of Health. You're disturbing the neighbors, he said. I understand, I said. Yes, said the inspector, they complain that they can't sleep. It seems it's so quiet in here that the people in the neighboring apartments can't sleep. They just lie there listening, wondering if they won't hear something soon.

That's a very peculiar charge, I said.

Yes, said the inspector, it is; I'm just doing my duty.

I got hold of a radio. I had it on all night so my neighbors would be able to sleep. I kept vigil through the nights and tuned in to foreign stations. I was exhausted when the inspector came and said that my neighbors couldn't sleep.

This time the charges are more serious, he said. Now you're disturbing them with noise. That's more in accord with our regulations.

I understand, I said. I took my buttons with "First names!" and "Be an optimist!" and pinned them on the inspector's chest. He took them off, shook his head and looked seriously worried.

A person has to keep track of when it's Friendliness Week and when it isn't Friendliness Week, he said.

I made sure that I ran into the leadership genius, the one who'd progressed further with his friendliness than anyone in the whole building, the one who was in first place for friendliness. Hi there, he said, what have you done with your buttons? I gave them away, brother, I answered, I gave them away to someone who needed them more than I did.

The leader made a friendly grimace.

I have understood, I said, I'm not the kind of person to miss a friendly hint – will you please find me another apartment.

I never refuse anyone a friendly favor, said the leader. That move should be easy to arrange, brother.

I sold what I had, as I'd done before, got other stuff, moved here.

Strange stories you tell, said Renkvist.

Yes, said Silberstein, they are strange stories.

He stood still, leaning against the wall, his face expressionless. Life is moods and every story becomes strange, he said.

If you should need help, Mr. Silberstein, said Renkvist, I don't think anyone would be able to help you.

No, said Silberstein, I'm sure no one could.

Renkvist felt solemn. I've gotten him to talk, he thought, that flatters my vanity as a journalist. It satisfies me enough to make me less aggressive toward the man. I feel a pleasant sympathy for him. I can go home to my wife and say that I've had a long talk with that man Silberstein. I think he felt it was nice to be able to get a load off his chest. I can allow myself that little lie, after all, if in fact it is a lie. She'll like the idea.

They lingered there in the stairwell. Renkvist felt that his feet were tired. Well, he said, trying to sound cheerful, the wife is waiting, good night, Mr. Silberstein.

I can imagine, said Silberstein, that you wonder why I go on living. I've already said that I'm usually afraid, and in that feeling there is no doubt a kind of life force.

He spoke thoughtfully, his voice rasping slightly with a soft, warm sound.

My eyes are on the ground, he continued, my head is heavy, but sometimes I yield to an overpowering desire to turn my face upwards. It's as if a pair of strong hands lifts my head and my stiff neck suddenly offers no resistance.

And then I too can experience a terrible pleasure. The cool night air touches my face and I travel through the infinite as a person sometimes can, and a different dimension brushes against me and passes through me with ease and I feel that I am delightfully lost.

He sighed heavily, the light went out, Renkvist heard him breathing in the dark, went and turned on the light. Silberstein had turned toward his door, he put the key in the keyhole, opened the door, disappeared into his place without a word.

Renkvist stood there for a moment looking at the closed door.

Life is moods, he muttered.

Then he shrugged and went upstairs to his place.

The cold morning light seemed to explode against his face.

Silberstein lay motionless for a while. Today too, he thought.

He raised his head slightly. Oh yes, the ache was there, like a disc pressing down inside his skull. Everything was just as it should be.

He got up carefully. Now he was standing beside the bed. It was going fine, he didn't need any support. He tugged a bit at his rumpled clothes, fumbling, indifferent – what did it matter how he looked? He went over to the sink, turned on the faucet, let it run for a while. Then he cupped his hands and scooped water up into his face. The water smarted on his dry skin, he took a little in his mouth and swallowed.

My God, he thought, today too. He moved slowly, aimlessly, around the apartment. A stroll without destination, as if to test his limbs. Old.

His memory roamed. He couldn't manage to control it. Images flickered by. Fragments of a life. Faces, rooms, gestures. He couldn't stop remembering.

He searched for an activity, looked around his rooms for something to do that would make the memories die down. He put coffee up to brew. Moved some bags around meaninglessly. Rubbed dust off a piece of furniture with his hand.

Dry mouth. Good God how I must have talked last night! Yes I did. I talked. Why did I have to talk.

Slowly he remembered what he had said. He was seized by anguish. Everything he had said seemed disastrous. Intrusive. He had been intrusive. He went over everything he had talked about. There was really nothing that was so terrible, he told himself. He tried to get himself to be reasonable, but every word he remembered was charged with mustiness and obscure risks.

He searched for Renkvist's face, but he couldn't find it, it didn't take on any contours, just slid away, he couldn't come up with anything.

He started. It was the coffee boiling over. He rushed to grab the pot. A few seconds of relief. Wiped up the coffee grounds. Busily cleaned the stove. Poured, took a sip and burned himself.

He spit into the sink. Hell, he thought, I'm much too awake, it shouldn't happen so abruptly.

His heart pounded. Sweat broke out on his forehead. Hung over again, he muttered and tried to grin at it, but it was strangely serious. This succession of days and nights, drunks and hangovers – what was he avoiding? Delayed-action defense, you might say. Rebound defense: let people get close to you in order to get rid of them.

But was it true? Had he really managed to bring this off – for either himself or the others? The ones he had rejected at once, the ones he had allowed to come a little further, perhaps too far.

His reason couldn't keep his panic under control. He saw eyes staring at him, but he couldn't read their expressions. He had really gone too far, he thought; he had made himself dependent.

What do you think of me, he suddenly howled.

The cry sank flat, there was no echo in the apartment.

He listened, frightened.

Where does this cry come from? Does it really matter to me what people think of me? Have I failed completely, then?

The eyes stared, expressionless. They looked at him. Everyone could see him. In the end there was no way to be invisible.

I'm of no concern to you, he said, and all at once his voice sounded steady and normal. He tried reaffirming it: It's really true, I'm of no concern to you. No one in the building, no one in the world is thinking of me now.

No one in the world is thinking of me, he repeated. He grew suddenly alert. Had it sounded like a complaint? Had a treacherous note of self-pity crept in?

What do I really want?

Why was he sweating like this? It certainly wasn't warm. He opened a window. He inhaled the morning air in deep breaths, overdoing it, until he had to cough. His body felt disgustingly damp. It's the hangover, he said, of course it's just the hangover. He struggled out of his jacket; sloping shoulders and potbelly, his shirt soiled, where can I hide? An unappetizing piece of life, that's what he was, should have an excellent chance of being left in peace. For that was, after all, what he wanted. It certainly was. And he was in peace. He was alone.

Why are they staring, then? And what kind of looks were those? Why didn't he dare to read their expressions?

What do you think of me?

What do you think of me, Miss Svensson, you with your fawning goodwill? What notions of my life and character do I inspire in you?

He chuckled.

He could hear her crackly old maid's voice. Was it crackly, come to think of it – wasn't it soft and warm?

I understand you so perfectly, Mr. Silberstein . . .

He repeated her words to himself. He gave them a menacing ring. But surely that didn't fit with her face? What was it she understood? Nothing, of course. The words were just a hollow gambit. Nothing to remember. Nothing to speculate about. People say good morning, they talk about the weather, they say they understand each other. And the morning isn't good all the same, it's raining, and people are blind and shut.

One understands nothing, but one always thinks something.

What do you think of me, Miss Svensson?

Oh, Mr. Silberstein, I think you are very lonely and very good. You seem good, and isolated, perhaps a shade misanthropic, Mr. Silberstein, that's understandable, after what you've gone through, such a hard fate, but one mustn't forget that deep down in every person there is something . . . yes, Mr. Silberstein, one mustn't lose faith in goodness, and I don't believe you've done so, either. I think that you, Mr. Silberstein, are such a . . .

What purpose did all this understanding have except to cram him full of other people's fantasies! And then subject him to the hostility of the disappointed. For he would never correspond to anyone's understanding of him. To dance like a marionette for other people's conceptions of you! That's something you can do when you're young and full of self-confidence. As long as you've still got a personality, you can bend with every whisper in your surroundings, but when you've relieved yourself of the whole burden of qualities you are stiff, you can't adapt anymore – for how can understanding describe you now. And the deepest pleasure of understanding is description.

That's how it is, he said aloud.

He slurped up some coffee. He'd started to feel cold. He was really shivering. And a moment ago he'd been sweaty. I don't feel well, he thought, maybe I have a fever. What if I'm seriously ill!

He put his jacket on. Ridiculous that he should be so scared of being sick. What would that matter?

Responsibilities, he chuckled. Promises. How will the hair-dressers put waves in their clients' hair! Promises made to be prompt with pomade.

Yes, he was sick for sure. Playing silly word games, at his age! I don't understand you, Mr. Silberstein . . .

No, Miss Svensson, I don't add up. Perhaps it isn't so hard to learn to add up, but I have trouble learning, and besides, I don't want to. I don't want to! Leave me before I start missing you!

Missing her! He couldn't control his thoughts. The ruts were worn smooth and the thoughts slipped into them.

He thought he heard Asp neighing.

That's fine, my dear Asp, he thought, go ahead and drivel at me, it feels good, give me some fine invectives, they're better than understanding. Reduce me to a distorted caricature, that's exactly as much description as I can take.

Let me have some ugly words to suit my ugly nose!

Dear Asp, you are kind and good to me, you don't think anything at all about me. You only see yourself and your glass, and you just use me so you can play the scoundrel. I'm a part of your ostentatious decline.

But why should I begin to enjoy you so much!

You spread poison in my veins and the poison's no sedative.

What expressions I'm using, he thought – the words of fever delirium and adventure stories . . .

Asp doesn't want anything from me. Asp doesn't think anything about me. He's fine. We used each other so splendidly a few times, but I can't even bring it off with Asp. I must be truly inept.

What do you want from me? What do you think of me?

Such a short time in this building and in this city and already those questions. He sat rocking lamely over his hopelessness.

What do you want from me? What do you think of me?

Loud this time. His voice and intonation implacably grinding, his breathing rapid and sharp. He got up, paced back and forth across the floor, arms swinging.

Shut yourself in, lock yourself up, pull down the shades! Your hat pulled down over your forehead when you go out, your head down, greet them or don't greet them! You catch a glimpse of their faces anyway, and soon you recognize them. You hear their voices on the stairs, you hear their calls and their greetings and soon you know their voices. And there they are, all around you, and they finger the plaque on the door and soon they know your name. And they see your face and recognize your footsteps.

What do you want from me? What do you think of me?

You mustn't think anything! You mustn't want anything! That's just the point of the whole thing. The goal of all my efforts. I obliterated myself, but you couldn't keep from filling this void with your fantasies: nothing attracts like a vacuum.

And therefore that journalist yesterday. My worst failure so far. The desire to act a part reawakening. The desire to look good. The desire to be remembered. That terrible, sweet pleasure when you feel another person's reactions vibrating all around you.

It's quite obvious that I'm inclined to dislike Jews . . .

Silberstein stopped in the middle of the floor.

Another person's reactions and then the responsibility . . . When one of you behaves badly I take it as a confirmation . . .

Silberstein put his hands in front of his face – O God, he muttered, O God. I who know fear so well . . . I'm afraid.

For a moment it was nice in there, in the darkness of his hands. Filthy Jew, Jewish swine, he heard dear Asp's strident voice. I'm a Judeophile . . . Listen to curses and invectives, feel liberated. The relief of persecution . . .

Tell your persecution stories to that journalist so maybe he won't push the responsibility-button anymore.

Coquetry, that storytelling voice. I strike poses. I'm affected. I act a part. I am responsibly appealing. I'm falling.

He took his hands away from his face and started pacing again. His boots creaked in the silence.

I am someone in the building. What do you want from me? What do you think of me? I want to get away from here.

He went over to the window. He looked down at the street and imagined it was full of people looking up at him. It seemed to him that they were shouting at him. He shut the window, shut out their cries. He saw their gaping mouths and some of them shook their fists at him.

Tell me what I've done, he said, lifting his hands and shrugging.

But he couldn't hear their answers.

There were more and more of them, they became a crowd, he saw their upturned faces packed together and all the red throats.

Go away, he screamed, get out of here!

The street was empty. It had been empty all along.

He missed them. Why didn't they come – he was standing here missing them, wasn't he?

He moved away from the window.

He mustn't stand there missing them! What was he getting himself into? What was he being pulled toward?

He stood where he was, a few steps into the room, with his shoulders hunched up and his arms hanging down, his head shaking, his eyes shut. Then he raised his hands to his head, moved them slowly downward over his temples, pressed hard; his rough hair felt dead against his palms.

Those Jews who have succeeded in keeping their qualities intact have been virtually heroic . . .

As for me, I just ended up with the fear.

I've plucked myself bare of everything but my fear.

So come here and hit me! Because the fear also wants to have its due. Time for the next Crusade. Time for the next Holy War.

But on my account all the others should be spared. Where does that strange idea come from? I will fill your need to see terrified eyes – and you can leave all the Maccabees alone. All those who really are bold and skillful, good and excellent. Peculiar idea!

Oh no, Emanuel Silberstein, you're not going to slip out of it through that back door. When one of you behaves badly I take it as a confirmation.

But if the terror in my eyes were to make them ashamed. . . .

What's the matter with you, Emanuel Silberstein, have you begun to have faith in people? Are you going to rely on their sense of shame?

He was still standing in the same rigidly cramped position. His hands worked at his temples but gave no relief. No, he was not getting out of it. He was standing in the middle of this building and trembling and around him there buzzed all the intentions and interpretations that he could not get at.

It's time for you to go to work now, he tried.

He started laughing uncontrollably. It sounded like hiccups: the cramps changed everything.

I feel strange, he said, this condition is completely unnatural to me.

But it wasn't true. He could recognize himself in all of it – in every bit of this old used-up body, every twist in these old used-up thoughts. He stood there feeling all this and for a moment he was almost at peace.

Alone.

But the stubborn cry rose up in him.

What do you want from me? What do you think of me?

And once again he saw all their faces – curious. They came so close to him that he could feel their breath.

He had to open his eyes to get rid of them.

The daylight stung his eyes. He blinked. And suddenly he yawned. I'm tired, he thought, I'm actually sleepy.

Oh no, don't try that, Emanuel Silberstein! You're awake, horribly awake. That's right, rub your eyes a little and you'll feel how awake you are. The windows are dirty, but not too dirty for you to see that it's day, and that it's a very long time until evening. You have one whole, long, blessed workday in front of you. Yes, try to joke a little about it. Kid a little about your work, Emanuel, or have a little talk with Papsi about it, how it's good enough to make a living from and is refreshingly free of any other significance.

I'm trying to see you, Papsi, but I've gotten such a crowd of people around me in this building. I live in the here and now. I've made acquaintances. People have gotten to know me, I have my circle, you see. What they're like? I don't know, but I'm sure they're nice. Whether they appreciate me? I don't know, how am I supposed to know that, what do you expect of me?

What they think of me?

So you've come to that now too! Do you really think it matters so much? You think so, do you. Oh, that's awful.

Should I go out and find out about it? Should I ring at all the doors and ask? It won't work, because in behaving that way you change their views. You see how impossible it is.

And I have no role I can act for them. I have in fact no view of myself that I can force on them. Describe me, Papsi!

Yes, you see how impossible it is now. You search for words, you get vague. It's not so easy to make clear to them that I was rather nice and rather happy now and then when I was little. Try something else!

Honest! Well. . . . But not for terribly noble reasons. Habit, caution and so on. That's nothing to ring doorbells about.

Ugly. That much they've already seen for themselves.

Have I made you laugh? Funny, then. Now there's something I don't think they've understood. Maybe I can be the building's funnyman. For that you don't need any personality. In fact it works best without one. Because comics really aren't anything but what they say. Maybe that was a very good suggestion.

I'm going to take a few days and go through the joke section in the papers. The only trouble is that everyone reads the same papers and the best jokes are in the ones with the biggest circulations.

O God, the mailbox banged! No mail, he knew, just the children, those happy little pranksters! This whole building was chock-full of kids and adults and adults and kids, there was no end to them. It was overpopulated, and here he stood in the middle of the floor in an almost empty two-room apartment, alone without ever being able to have some peace! Voices, steps on the stairs, a restless activity, an incessant buzzing as in a beehive. And him locked up here. He had to get going now, he had to get out. He had to pass by all the doors, all the voices, all the faces.

What do you want from me? What do you think of me?

I have to know what they want from me! I have to know what they think of me!

And if they don't want anything? If they don't think anything?

Then I'll have to make them know what they want from me! I'll have to make them know what they think of me!

He took his coat and hat. He was in a hurry, had a hard time getting his arms into the coat, pressed the hat down over his forehead. He rushed to the door, got it open, banged it shut behind him.

The stairway was empty. He stood completely still, breathing hard, his back against the door, protected. The only sound was the slam of his own door still ringing in his ears.

O God, where are all the people? What are they up to?

Where are all of you, he shouted.

It was silent.

I need your persecution!

He started trembling. Why have you forsaken me? Come to me! Come after me!

He wanted to start down the stairs, but his legs wouldn't obey, he couldn't move. Time had stopped, everything had stopped. It seemed to him he was standing there inhaling eternity in short, labored breaths, it burned his heart, and his heart burned up and he had only a lump of ash in his breast.

It'll soon be over now, he thought. This can't go on, soon everything will change. But still everything was completely quiet, there was only the lump of ash pounding away, he thought the whole world must be able to hear it.

His face began to itch, but his hands were so heavy that he couldn't manage to lift them. It won't itch very long, he thought, it'll pass soon if only I can stop thinking about it. Just don't scratch, Mammi used to say. If you don't scratch, it passes – that was a good rule.

You had so many good rules and now I'm standing here and can't move – can you give me a rule, Mammi?

Hi, old Jew!

It was a little girl who was suddenly standing there and giving him a friendly smile, he didn't know if he had seen her before, there were so many of them, after all, and he never looked at them.

You don't look happy, she said.

He shook his head, moved one hand up to his face and scratched, he could move again.

I'm happy, said the girl. I got a new jump rope.

She showed him. He smiled carefully at her.

Though I'm not good at jumping rope. I'm still too little. Why are you standing here? Are you waiting for someone?

I've been waiting for you, he said.

You mean you knew I would come?

I know now.

Yes, he knew the whole thing. He listened tensely for sounds coming up the stairway. Still no steps.

Now you mustn't be afraid, he said softly. Promise me.

Why should I be afraid?

No reason, he said. I'm not going to scare you. But you're going to help me very nicely.

With what?

You won't understand that.

Still no steps on the stairs. He held the girl there with his smile. He hoped she wouldn't get frightened. That was the only responsibility he felt now. It would go easily enough.

They're going to know what they want, he said. They're going to know what they think.

Who do you mean, she asked.

The whole thing is very stupid, you understand, he said sadly. I'm very frightened, you see. And I'm finally going to know why.

Still silent. He felt with alarm that the cramps were about to come back. He started sweating.

I want to go now, said the girl.

Wait a bit, he asked. Just a little while. You'll see that it'll go very fast.

What's going to go very fast?

He started. He thought the entrance door had banged.

They'll be here right away, he whispered. He heard the steps getting closer. Soon they'd turn the corner, in a moment the person coming first would see him up here on the landing.

Now you must show me your panties. He bent forward and slowly lifted the girl's skirt.

The child's laugh and the woman's scream came at the same instant.

Run along, he whispered.

Then he let panic grip him. He couldn't get his keys out. He heard more screams and shouts. Doors began slamming.

Deathly scared, he started tearing up the stairs. Panic gave him speed and strength.

He heard running steps.

And in the midst of the fear his thoughts were strangely clear and calm.

Finally, he thought, I have renounced responsibility for all the others and taken on my own suffering.

He continued upward, upward.

He heard them shouting to one another.

They were finally hunting him.

12

They watched him sitting at the extreme edge of the roof, and they didn't keep track of how long they had been watching him sit there. Now and then he had stood up, and they had all cried out. Then he had stood there awhile and stared downwards and upwards and they had all been amazed that he didn't get dizzy. When he later sat down again they all sighed, and then they discovered that no one had said a word for a long time, and then they began talking. The fire company was there now with ladders and a net, and the police, but as soon as they set a ladder up near him or approached in any other way, he stood up so they had no choice but to retreat.

He'll have to calm down first, the firemen and policemen said, and everyone had just gone back to waiting.

If they don't jump right away they don't jump at all, said the firemen professionally. What the hell kind of character is he, anyway?

Schoolmaster Olausson, who was standing near the fire captain, informed him that it was a morals offender. Little girls, he said in a low voice. He didn't want too many people to hear him, he knew what primitive reactions such information called forth in some people – he himself did not have that sort of primitive moralistic instinct and the fire captain looked like an educated man.

Oh hell, drawled the captain; he didn't sound particularly interested. Olausson felt misunderstood, as well as indignant over how morally indifferent some people were.

As it turned out, nothing happened, thank God. Someone came up the stairs, Olausson explained, and the girl didn't understand a thing. I just showed him my panties, she said and laughed. Thank God.

And then you chased him up onto the roof, said the captain.

Me – said Olausson angrily – I wasn't even home when it happened.

No, of course not, said the captain, it's always like that.

Olausson understood that he'd been mistaken about the fire captain. He was a coarse and uncivilized man, as well as morally indifferent. But then, the main thing, after all, was that he could put out fires.

For a moment Olausson felt a little restorative contempt for the art of putting out fires.

He walked over to Renkvist, the journalist, who was standing a short distance away and singlemindedly staring up at Silberstein.

Yes, said Olausson with a little laugh of shared understanding, it's funny to see how much sense a behavior pattern makes when one gets a glimpse of the outcome.

In his opinion he said this rather modestly.

We have now found an explanation for that man's behavior up to the present, he continued.

What's happened here doesn't in the least add up the way you think, said Renkvist angrily. Moreover it's not one bit funny.

He moved away from Olausson so he could be alone with himself and Silberstein.

He was tired and extremely tense. His neck ached from holding his head back at an awkward angle, his eyes ached from all the staring. In addition, he had lain up there on the roof for a long while and tried to bring Silberstein to his senses.

He had climbed up through the roof hatch and seen the flapping black silhouette over at the edge of the roof. He hadn't dared to crawl closer.

Halloo, Silberstein, he'd called out cautiously.

Silberstein started and for a moment it seemed as if he was going to fall.

Sit down, Silberstein, he called.

Silberstein remained standing.

You can hear me, he called. Silberstein, I know that you can hear me! Sit down!

No answer. Now he was standing completely still.

Renkvist had lain there awhile in silence, desperate, unable to find words, not daring to move closer, not daring to leave.

There was some wind up there, Silberstein's coat was flapping, but the wind wasn't strong. Up here the building seemed like a tower, because everything around it had been torn down.

I won't come any closer even if you sit down, he called out on the far side of the silence that had seemed unbearably long.

The man over at the edge stood there for a while without moving, Renkvist thought he was swaying slightly but wasn't sure. He must be weary now, he thought, and then he saw him sit down, very cautiously.

That's right, Silberstein, he called. He felt ridiculously triumphant.

It'll work out, he had thought. Now all I have to do is continue.

Think it out, he called. Think everything through one more time. No matter how you look at it, this has to be unnecessary.

Silberstein looked as if he'd been listening, but Renkvist couldn't be certain.

You haven't done anything, after all, he called. I don't think you intended to do anything either.

Silberstein had turned his head slightly to one side; Renkvist imagined he'd done it so he could hear better.

I don't believe that about you, he called out. No one who's met you will believe that about you.

At that Silberstein stood up violently – now he's falling, Renkvist thought when he heard the screams from down in the street, but the old man remained standing at the edge.

Up there in the wind Renkvist felt how he'd begun to sweat. For Chrissake, he screamed in full panic, if you're going to kill yourself then do it a little less dramatically, there are children down there, do you have to make them watch this? Give it up and find some other method!

Some other method, he thought – the old man has been chased up here, after all; his choice is between living and jumping. I must have said something wrong, seeing that he got up again.

Then he had suddenly gotten tremendously mad.

And it was you who didn't want to be noticed, he screamed. Now you've sure as hell seen to it that you'll be remembered! I hope you're satisfied now! Life is moods! Well change your mood, goddammit! Or jump right into the gang of kids down there!

He had lain there screaming like that, stupidly and inconsistently, until he'd finally seen Silberstein sit down again. Then he started crying from tension and relief. He lay there crying for a while up on the roof, and then he thought he'd better come down, he didn't trust his ability to cope with this thing.

I'm leaving now, Silberstein, he had called. Think it out!

And now he was standing down here and staring up at the figure at the edge of the roof. Next to him his wife stood gaping foolishly and there were two large holes behind her glasses. It mustn't happen, she mumbled from time to time, it mustn't come to that. He looked at her dry cheeks that could be so soft and felt strangely guilty.

You shouldn't stand here, he said in as friendly a tone as he could. Why don't you go inside.

I can't, she muttered, oh good God this mustn't happen.

It seemed to her that she didn't have a single thought in her head except that it mustn't happen. That thought and a thousand images. The image of him standing and sitting at the edge of the roof, the image of him falling – this she saw both from here and from her window, the body dancing past on its merciless way downward, which she would never be able to see from her window, it didn't face that way. And then images of him the times when she'd met him, and images of him as she imagined he was when she couldn't see him, and all these images were so incredibly vivid that she had to mutter the whole while that it mustn't happen. And then images of him lying dead and broken, the last, definitive distortion that life would treat him to, the body in all kinds of twisted positions and the shattered face and she didn't care about anything except that this mustn't happen.

The voices around her seemed strangely distant. She stood there quite alone among the others. She heard Brundin's hoarse voice near her but she didn't care what it was saying.

Of course we ran after him, said Brundin. Naturally. The way they were screaming, and then when we heard what he'd done or was going to do. Of course we ran.

He spoke slowly, as if he were defending himself, though no one had attacked him, or as if he were thinking something through.

I thought, I'll get him against the attic door, he continued, but the attic door was ajar and I searched awhile until I saw the roof hatch and then I understood, and the others who were with me understood too, and we ran down into the street, but he hadn't jumped. He still hasn't jumped.

He said it as if it were news.

And the girl was still standing there on the stairs, he said slowly, she was laughing the same way when we ran down as when I first saw her on the way up. The whole thing seemed very odd.

It can't have been wrong of us to try to get hold of him, after all.

The whole thing happened so fast.

I've never thought that there was anything wrong with him.

Brundin spoke with long pauses. It seemed as if he was thinking through what he was saying very carefully.

That's too godawful – with little girls, he said vehemently.

Then a pause.

Next: Though what the hell does that have to do with this here. But you hear them shouting, and you run. That's how it is.

If only we'd gotten hold of him nothing would have happened, he said. He sensed that what he was saying sounded illogical, but he knew perfectly well what he meant.

It was nice to meet him on the stairs now and then, he said helplessly. But you hear them shouting, and you run.

He fell silent. His fat wife stood next to him, assiduously and mechanically stroking his arm while she looked upwards, keeping her eyes glued on Silberstein.

There there, there there, she said continuously.

And the whole while she could hear the thin woman's shrill voice grinding away next to her. I saw it I did, I actually saw it with my own eyes, I saw what was about to happen. That hideous person, that hideous man – I've always thought he was hideous. And shady. Shady. Just that! This is exactly what you'd expect from him. I've been waiting for this to happen. And that poor, poor girl! Marked for life. The schoolmaster says that things like this leave scars that last a lifetime! I was the one who saw it. God only knows how it would have ended if I hadn't come along. But we know very well how it would have ended. Naked and bleeding! We've read about such things. Lucky I got hold of her mother! She had a shock, poor woman! In there weeping now. Mother and child both in shock. The kid just laughed, she was so out of her wits! And no wonder! An experience like that! I was the one who made black coffee for her mother. I gave the kid some juice. What's a person to do? Little children shouldn't have coffee. Just forget all about that ugly old man, I said. Forget him, sweetie! She's just like a little doll. And to be molested by someone like that! What did he do to you, I asked. Nothing, she said. Can you imagine – Nothing, she said, didn't know any better, kids don't understand anything but that's why they get in trouble! But when she saw her mother crying, then of course she understood that something horrible had happened to her and she started crying too, the poor kid. And there I was running back and forth, pouring coffee into the mother and juice into the little girl – praise God it didn't end up the other way around, I was so mixed up by the horrible thing that had happened and could happen to your own children the way things are nowadays. I hear he's a Jew too. Yes, you see! The kind of people we're letting in! My knees are still shaking. Imagine if there hadn't been anyone in the building to hear me screaming – because I was the one who screamed. And now he's standing up there and I hope he won't dare to jump because his kind should just be locked up as fast as you can get hold of them – not that he'll dare to jump, they never dare because they're cowards, cowards . . .

It was a stream of words that never let up. The woman's hair was a mess and she looked frightened to death and everyone understood that she didn't dare to stop talking.

That thing isn't true, thought Miss Svensson over and over, it isn't true, I know it isn't true. They all think that I'm an old maid who doesn't understand anything and most especially not something like this, but I know it isn't true because I've looked him in the eye. I can almost say that I know Mr. Silberstein, oh he's such a charming man, cultured and refined, we've had such good, such full conversations with each other. A bit difficult to get to know, perhaps, but that's often the case with people who have a rich inner life. Oh, Mr. Silberstein, not so close to the edge, you might fall!

Frightened, she quickly opened her umbrella as a parachute, so powerfully that the ribs thrust aside the people standing close to her and she ended up inside a wide circle, lonely, sad, ridiculous under her open umbrella.

No, I'll go in, she thought, confused – I'm not doing any good here, poor man, I'm really no help to him. And why should I stand here staring at him, maybe he wants to be in peace up there on the roof.

Mr. Silberstein, she called. I'm going inside now, but I'll be thinking of you all the time.

But he looked as if he hadn't heard this at all, and no doubt he hadn't, it was so terribly far to shout, after all, and her voice wasn't strong.

And with her umbrella held high so as not to stab anyone with those nasty points on the ribs, she went into the building.

That's what we should all do, thought Renkvist, we should go away and leave him in peace. But he stayed.

He thought about how it had been in the beginning. Silberstein at the edge of the roof and many people yelling dirty words up at him and shaking their fists, and suggestions that they go up and shove him over if he didn't have enough decency left in his body to be able to jump on his own. He thought about how a few people had enjoyed trying to keep the volatile mood alive but how, gradually, more and more people had understood that they would be forced to see the body broken on the pavement and had begun to be afraid of that sight. And the longer they looked at the man up there the more palpable he became for them and the more they doubted that they really could stand to see him jump.

And they had all lowered their voices.

And he thought about how, after coming down from the roof, he had stood looking up at Silberstein and had suddenly felt very aggressive and thought he'd damned well better make up his mind soon, I can't stand here all day, I'm starting to get hungry goddammit!

And had later been ashamed of thinking that.

And Olausson, having thought out a witticism, had come over to him and said that that man's behavior pattern was truly no pattern for behavior. If you get what I mean?

And then he had felt even more ashamed, though it couldn't have been on his own behalf.

And then a voice next to him. That's what the whole lot of us should do. That's the best thing you can do for yourself in this world – jump off a roof. Find yourself a plausible pretext and then jump. That's the best thing.

Someone bitter.

And other voices. Sweetheart, it's too nasty! Yes when you think that we may have children of our own someday. But you can't help feeling sorry for him too. Not me. But they can't help it. And he's so lonely. He doesn't have anyone. You shouldn't be standing here watching this, my pet. But I have to be with you, sweetheart. It's too nasty . . .

Renkvist had moved around. Voices everywhere. He tried to recall the conversation he'd had with Silberstein in the night, but he couldn't remember one word, he was distracted everywhere he went. What's more, he didn't dare to take his eyes off the scare-crow up there. He felt as if he were holding Silberstein back at the edge of the roof by looking at him – as soon as he looked away he would fall. Of course this was unreasonable, but that's how he felt. He hardly dared to blink. He found himself in a state of unbear-able, frantic concentration.

Voices. He'll be down soon now. One way or the other. My guess is the stairs. That's not exactly a hero up there. Some of them are brave. You can read about that. The way things were in those camps. Yes you've probably read about it. Some of them were heroes. But this one! A regular little wholesaler-Jew. Scared and perverted. My guess is the stairs.

They would place bets if they didn't have such a well-devel-oped sense of propriety, thought Renkvist. But if he stands up there long enough they'll put aside their good-mannered masks and then I'll have to listen to odds and amounts. And after that it won't take long before they're putting bills in a hat.

And whoever loses will have had a fire lit under his anti-Semitism. Life's a fine mess.

He giggled, felt his wife grasp his arm hard. I'm starting to get hysterical, he thought, soon I'll be standing here laughing my head off, and at that instant he heard a horselaugh next to him.

Hell of a note, snorted Asp, and no one saw how much terror there was in his eyes. What sort of games is the old Jew up to now, hm? He cupped his hands in front of his mouth and yelled. Hi there, Silversteen, it's your lowly servant Asp hailing your highness! Are you going to give us a circus act? Do a swan dive, old boy!

Someone took hold of Asp's arm; it was a policeman. You're leaving here, he said. Oh, said Asp, twisting free, I know that old guy very well, I know how to get him down. The policeman gave way, hesitantly.

Silversteen, yelled Asp, take the quickest route to old Asp now, come on and jump and I'll treat you to a round! Come here and we'll have a little talk about the Jewish question! I've got some juicy new words for you.

He's not reacting, said the policeman.

The patrolman can be goddamned sure that he is too, said Asp.

Silversteen, he yelled, that stuff's not for the likes of you and me. That's for respectable people. To hell with the circus act!

I'm going to laugh you off the block if you jump!

At that Renkvist looked away from Silberstein and regarded Asp. His mouth was drawn into a loose smile, he had one hand in his pants pocket, the other hand held a cigarette with studied elegance. His raised eyebrows made him look a trifle silly. Just a minute ago, thought Renkvist, he had his hands cupped like a megaphone, and now this nonchalant pose – he must be awfully scared.

Silversteen, screamed Asp, be a good boy now and take the stairs – your dear Asp doesn't want any Jew-blood spattering his fancy clothes!

Asp's eyes began to roam. He probably wanted to know what sort of impression he was making. All around him people stood in silence.

Old Jew, he screamed, I think I've stolen the scene from you, you're not up to this one, there's not a soul here who believes you, that's just lousy theater. I envy you your staging, but Jesus Christ what cheap acting!

Are you playing persecuted, Jew bastard?

Renkvist punched him right in the face. First Asp was completely startled and then he began to cry. I don't want him to jump, you know, he whimpered.

At that instant the crowd suddenly screamed again. Then dead silence.

I should never have taken my eyes off him, Renkvist thought, and slowly turned his face upwards, afraid of hearing a new scream.

Silberstein had gotten up again.

He stood there looking down. For a moment Renkvist thought he had met Silberstein's gaze, though of course he knew that it ought to be impossible at this distance. Now he'll get dizzy and fall, he thought, he's going to fall right on my face.

And suddenly the whole thing no longer seemed real to him. It's because I can't take any more, he thought. He tried to think about the ambulance, the fire company, the police, everyone who was there, to get back his sense of reality, but the ghostly, shameful silence swaddled him in this numbing dreaminess. I have to scream to wake myself up, he thought, but he couldn't get out a sound. Everything had come to a standstill around him and the image of the man up there at the edge of the roof had frozen on his retinas.

He could just barely make out that Silberstein was slowly raising his head.

Around him, silence.

They all stood there and waited.

Sometimes they stirred down there in a funny way. Sometimes they stood completely still.

Just now they were standing completely still.

He wasn't cold and he wasn't dizzy.

He didn't have many thoughts in his head. Anxiety came over him now and then, but he didn't have to wait long before it receded again.

Part of the time he had spent sitting down. When the anxiety came he had gotten up.

Just now he was standing up.

The sky was a very light blue, almost white.

He had a strange feeling of power. As soon as he got up they became very still and quiet down there.

And above him, stillness and silence.

He had no feeling of urgency.

He had heard Renkvist shouting to him on the roof, he had heard Asp yelling down there. They had made him anxious.

But all he'd had to do was get up.

He could see a long way off. He could remember a long way back. Everything seemed to be in its place now.

This was exactly how things should be.

This was his place, at the extreme edge of the roof.

He buttoned up his coat, huddled deeper into his clothes, smoothed them down over his body for a moment.

He made himself completely alone.

He waited.

He was waiting for a decision.

Jews seldom take their own lives, he thought, standing at the extreme edge of the roof, and was still undecided whether he would jump or not.